"This tastes wonderful," Diedre said, peeling another piece of meat off the spit.

Remembering how Sterling had gone about feeding her the night before, she teased his lips with it while slowly tracing her tongue around her own. "My turn," she murmured as seductively as she could manage, hoping he wouldn't notice that her fingers were beginning to shake.

He stared at her hard, in a most unnerving way. Then suddenly, in a swift flash of movement, she felt his grip on her wrist. She was too stunned to do more than stare back. His eyes turned an ominous shade of earth mixed with steel.

Her hand was so close to his mouth she could feel his harsh, ragged breath. Her mind constricted to pinpoint focus, until she was aware of nothing but the scent, the feel, and the frightening power of this dangerous man.

Commanding her wrist, he slowly moved it forward. The meat disappeared into his mouth at the moment she felt the touch of his lips. His mouth closed over her fingers, and she began to breathe again, too shallowly, too fast. She tried to stifle the moan in her throat, but failed.

"Careful, Diedre," he warned softly. "Be *very* careful before you tease me like that again. We're all alone. . . ." He nipped the tips of her fingers. "And, darlin', I like to bite. . . ."

WHAT ARE *LOVESWEPT* ROMANCES?

They are stories of true romance and touching emotion. We believe those two very important ingredients are constants in our highly sensual and very believable stories in the *LOVESWEPT* line. Our goal is to give you, the reader, stories of consistently high quality that may sometimes make you laugh, sometimes make you cry, but are always fresh and creative and contain many delightful surprises within their pages.

Most romance fans read an enormous number of books. Those they truly love, they keep. Others may be traded with friends and soon forgotten. We hope that each *LOVESWEPT* romance will be a treasure—a "keeper." We will always try to publish

LOVE STORIES YOU'LL NEVER FORGET
BY AUTHORS YOU'LL ALWAYS REMEMBER

The Editors

Loveswept® 507

Olivia Rupprecht
Date with the Devil

BANTAM BOOKS
NEW YORK · TORONTO · LONDON · SYDNEY · AUCKLAND

DATE WITH THE DEVIL

A Bantam Book / November 1991

If you would be interested in receiving protective vinyl
covers for your Loveswept books, please write to this address
for information:

Loveswept
Bantam Books
P.O. Box 985
Hicksville, NY 11802

ISBN 0-553-44143-4

Published simultaneously in the United States and Canada

Bantam Books are published by Bantam Books, a division
of Bantam Doubleday Dell Publishing Group, Inc. Its trademark, consisting of the words "Bantam Books" and the
portrayal of a rooster, is Registered in U.S. Patent and
Trademark Office and in other countries. Marca Registrada.
Bantam Books, 666 Fifth Avenue, New York, New York
10103.

PRINTED IN THE UNITED STATES OF AMERICA

OPM   0 9 8 7 6 5 4 3 2 1

For Keith McCleod McInnis—
an old salt who taught his Livy Ann
the art of making WWII SOS.
It wasn't the only dish he served up
with the promise that it would
put hair on my chest.

This book's for you, Daddy. Your spirit's
always close, but I sure miss your hugs.

One

"Breathe . . . damn you, *breathe!*"

Sterling Jakes cursed as more water rushed from the woman's slack, open mouth and onto the grainy white sand cushioning her cheek.

When the flow was less than a trickle, he rolled her limp, waterlogged body over. Working frantically against time, he quickly felt for a pulse. When he didn't find one, he began to pump on her solar plexis with the steady rhythm of his joined hands. He shifted to her mouth. With an impatient swipe he pushed away the loose strands of hair streaming over her face and fitted his lips over hers.

Cold, too cold, in spite of the harsh sun beating down on his back. He pinched her nose and exhaled into her mouth, trying to impart as much oxygen as he could without bursting her lungs like an overfilled balloon.

One . . . *Take my air, lady. Take it or you die.* He ignored the gritty texture of sand coating the vulnerable softness of their joined mouths.

Two . . . *Please, don't leave me stranded on this god-forsaken island all alone.* He could hear the squawk of gulls swooping down nearby to pick the rotting carcass of a shark the tide had washed up. Sterling's muscles bunched. Sharks—he could still feel them gaining speed, slicing razor-close, stalking him in lethal silence. That's when he'd lost his grip on the unconscious woman, and she'd gone under not seventy feet from shore.

Three . . . *C'mon, c'mon, give me a sign. One little breath, a cough, anything. I'll give up the smokes, I'll go to Confession, I'll quit drinking too much sake and beer and playing the ponies.*

She jerked on a spasm. A weak cough that tasted of salt water brought him upright on his haunches. And then another, a stronger one that turned into a violent fit as she wheezed and gasped for air.

He glanced up to the clear azure sky, an ironic smile twisting his lips. *Thanks. Forget what I said about Confession, but those other promises shouldn't be too hard to keep as long as we're stuck wherever the hell this is.*

Diedre felt as though she were swimming through a pool of quicksand. Each breath was a ragged struggle, grating against her raw throat. She thrashed against something wet, rough-textured, hot. What was wrong with her head? It was pounding so hard, she vaguely wondered if some maniac had gone berserk with a sledgehammer and cracked her skull. Her eyes were burning, and she couldn't pry them open. The ringing in her ears subsided to a low roar, and she thought she heard a man's distant voice.

"That's it, little darlin'," he said. "Just keep working those lungs like a newborn babe."

She could feel strong hands fitting beneath her arms and lifting her, then firmly patting her back while her aching chest pressed against something reassuring. She found the strength to touch that something, and decided it had hair, muscles, and must be male.

What was this? A vivid nightmarish scene from

one of her favorite books? It was definitely time for a vacation from the Fond du Lac library. Only wherever she was now, it wasn't there.

Diedre's eyes popped open. The immediate sting was too painful not to be real.

"Ohhh," she groaned around another cough. Shutting her eyes tightly against the blinding sun, she saw vivid lights dancing like a laser light show on her lids. "Please . . ." she whispered faintly. "Please, whoever you are, tell me . . . what happened, where . . . we are—"

"We're on a piece of land with water hugging us on all sides. As to what happened . . ." He paused, and she could feel his fingertips gently tracing her eyelids. "First, I want you to look at me. I know it'll hurt, but I need to check for damage. C'mon now, let me get a gander at those eyes."

Very slowly, Diedre pried her lids open. She was grateful that the man shielded her from the sun's glare with a cool hand bracketing her forehead. Her own arms felt leaden, too heavy to lift to do the same.

"You've got a gorgeous set of peepers, darlin'. Your pupils look good too. Now tell me how many fingers I'm holding up. Use those baby blues."

"Two? No . . ." She blinked, trying to focus. "One," she said with certainty. He held up several more fingers that even in her muddled state she recognized as large, dark, and capable. "Four."

"Very good." He smiled, and she was drawn to his face. "Okay," he said, "you passed the first test. Let's try out the memory banks. Do you remember where you're from?"

For a moment she couldn't. Her mind remained fixed on the striking set of masculine features before her. They were angular, with prominent cheekbones shaded by stubby whiskers beneath the dark hollows. A strong, square jaw harbored a dimpled cleft dipping into the jut of his chin. His lips drew tight in her continued silence. They were taut but full, a little too wide and generous.

"Oh, Lord," he groaned. "Think hard," he ordered. His voice had a raspy, sandpaper edge, and the urgency of it demanded her attention.

"Wisconsin," she answered while her gaze lifted to meet his eyes. Heavy brows that were slashes of dark brown flecked with gold matched his short, moist hair. His brows were like thick awnings over a pair of knowing hazel eyes. They were old eyes in a younger man's weathered face, which crinkled when he smiled his approval.

"You're a long way from home." He tilted his head, considering her. The flecks in his eyes showed a hint of blue and gray. "But then again," he added, "we both are at this point. Do you remember anything about this morning?"

She shook her head. Something dark threatened to surface in her memory, and she tried to catch the strand at the same time that her consciousness pushed it away.

"I . . ." She was still disoriented. Looking past the long slope of his bare shoulders, she was too astonished to wonder why he didn't have on a shirt. Diedre saw sand and more sand, the pristine whiteness giving way to a stand of palms. The trees reached upward, then bent forward as though the jungle behind them were pushing to get past their guardian gates. Palmettos and ivy and banana trees all fought for space while they merged into a breathtaking medley that was untamed and exquisite, savage and lush.

She remembered it was early March. Snow still covered patches of ground in Wisconsin. The stark contrast broke through her drifting thoughts.

"I won the contest from the travel agency," she suddenly whispered. Her gaze flew to the man. "I'm on vacation. The Bahamas. I . . . I left the hotel alone—"

"And you took a cruise with three other people on a Monday in the off-season."

"I remember you now." Her throat tightened painfully, and her stomach knotted. "You were taking notes while an older couple took pictures." The camera of her mind came into focus, clear and concise. She could feel the weathered wooden rail beneath her palm, could see herself covertly glancing at the man who now loomed large in her vision and was tightening his grip on her shoulders.

"You remember the lightning, the fog rolling in and the captain trying to outrun it—"

"Yes, yes! And then he yelled at us that he was getting only static on the radio but he was trying to send out an SOS anyway, that we needed to hurry and get the life jackets on. I can still see the waves, the boat—"

She could feel the damp fog and surging water. She could taste her own fear in her mouth as she scrambled for the life jacket while the small boat pitched sideways and she screamed in confusion and terror.

"Where are the others?" She latched on to him, shaking.

"No one else has washed up yet," he said gently. "Maybe they got their jackets on in time." His expression told her otherwise. "When we started tipping over, I grabbed the closest person—and that happened to be you."

She stared at him in shock. Her mouth worked, but only a strangled moan of denial found its way out.

"Easy," he said, "easy, now. You've had a bad time, but we're alive. Now hang on to me tight—that's a girl—and lay your head on my shoulder, just like that. I want to get you out of this sun before that fair skin burns even more. You're gonna hurt like hell by tonight, but at least you'll still be around to hurt."

She felt him gather her into his arms. Strong arms. She clung to them while her mind pitched and swayed as violently as the capsizing boat had.

"How did it happen?" she asked faintly, wanting to forget, to go home, to be anywhere but here. She willed her mind to drift away as he began walking, the steady thump of her cheek against his neck matching the beat of her heart.

"Take it from an old salt, darlin'," he said next to her ear. "Anything can happen in the Bermuda Triangle. When you take a date with The Devil, it's a whole new set of rules."

With each step he took, she slipped farther from consciousness' shore until reality and faded dreams mingled and she knew only darkness, merciful and sweet.

Sterling stared down at the young woman sleeping on the bed of palm leaves. Foliage was dense and provided good cover, but there was enough light from the dipping sun for him to see the face and form he'd touched and labored to save.

Now that he was assured she was going to live, he could appreciate the fine, feminine lines stretched out full length before him. The mouth he'd breathed into was full. Though her lips still looked parched from thirst, they were almost as inviting as his first glimpse of land after what he figured was well over a ten-mile swim.

Her tangled hair, coming loose from its braid, was dry, and he saw that it was a light shade of honey, the kind that was rich and warm, like a tall bourbon without ice. He was a sucker for long hair, long legs, and a pretty face.

He wasn't one for temperance, and the fact that she

owned all three of his favorite assets sparked his libido with more than a little gusto. She looked young and innocent lying there, healthy and fresh. She no longer resembled the prim, reserved young lady he'd immediately noticed on the boat. With her sun-burned skin she certainly looked far from the frail dishrag the sea had miraculously spit out before snuffing.

From her youthful features, now without makeup, he guessed she was twenty-two or twenty-three, at least twelve years younger than he was. She had freckles over a fine, upturned nose, cheekbones a skier could coast down at top speed, and wide-spaced eyes so blue they were almost violet. They'd had an impact on him, close to a well-thrown punch or a groin kick students practiced at one of the martial-arts *dojos* he owned in the Florida Keys. She might be half his size, but those big baby blues lent her the advantage over the red-blooded instincts he could feel heating up.

Sterling took a ragged, deep breath. The tighten-ing of his jeans caused the Swiss Army knife in his pocket to press against his hip. He'd been called an animal before, *moko tora*—fierce tiger—by the Grand-master. It had been a supreme compliment, but standing here now, lusting after this girl's vulnerable sweetness, he knew there was nothing honorable in this facet of his animal nature.

The waywardness of his reaction had him wishing for a pack of Camels and a bottle of Coors. Besides the green beret his mother proudly displayed over her mantel, they were his most lingering reminders of the military—kind of like a bad woman who made a man feel too good. He knew he should give them up, but even if the spirit was willing, the body wasn't buying it.

The girl sighed and shifted, causing her white blouse to ride up her stomach and her matching pants to inch down, exposing a small, sexy mole. Sterling swallowed hard, while his gaze took inventory.

Neck—arched back and pale; it wasn't hard to imagine kissing his way down. Breasts—as round and firm as the coconuts he'd just culled; almost tasting them, he knew they would be as sweet as the fruit's milk. Hips—generous, but not too generous, deliciously curved and full. Legs—his lips let go of a long whistle.

All in place—*definitely* all in place, he decided. Her arms, splayed over her head, were like the rest of her body: slender but muscular enough to suggest strength. Good, he thought with approval; he needed a strong partner for what possibly lay ahead.

Her clothes were ripped but alluring. He supposed the tears came from the jolt of being capsized or from his less than gentle handling during their ordeal. Swimming, towing, just him and this woman and sky kissing the sea . . . and then, miraculously, *land*. Blessed land. Escaping the sharks by a prayer, staggering to the shore, then nearly collapsing on top of her as soon as his bare feet touched damp sand.

He impulsively dropped to his knees in thanks. He kissed the ground, grateful to have been spared, grateful his expert skills had given them a second chance. As Sterling looked up, his eyes encountered the nakedness of a small, pale waist and the slight indentation of her navel.

Just beneath the swell of her breasts was the area he'd pumped while pleading for her heart to beat. His hand hovered over her, but even without touching, he could feel her body heat, could imagine the gentle slope filling his palm.

He felt a quickening. Primal. Exciting. Intense.

He'd saved this woman, and he couldn't deny his heroics were culminating in some damn selfish thoughts. The aching male need, strong as the instinct to drink and eat, took hold with a gripping urgency. It pulsed against his temples and tightened his throat, then moved down to expand between his thighs.

"Whoever you are, the Fates rolled the dice, and tossed our lots together," he said in a whisper. "I don't know if what we've shared today is causing it, or the chance we could grow old before we're discovered . . . but I need to feel your soft, warm body giving me a little peace." He pressed his lips to her forehead. "You belong to yourself. Why do I feel like you're mine?"

"*Jakes-san.*" Sterling heard the windsong of the Orient, filtered through an old man's familiar voice. "*Onushi dekiruna—you know when another has something special, and you draw together as old souls meeting in new life. As father to son, teacher to student, lover to lover, or friend to friend. Is it not wise then to listen with your heart? It hears much better than man's ears. Kamae, Jakes-san, is the body's way of speaking what has no words or form because it is held within the heart.*"

The woman muttered something incoherent. Sterling's inward gaze turned outward and rested on her face. Dusk was descending, casting on her shadows of magenta and vivid purple hues.

His hands gravitated to her hair, and he pulled two bands loose, then shoved them into his pocket. They might need these later, but for now he knew only the need to sift his fingers through the long braid and arrange her loose hair in a halo about her head.

"Sleep, darlin'," he said intimately. "Sleep so I won't have to apologize or explain.

"*Onushi dekiruna.*" Sterling touched his forefinger to his tongue, then pressed the wet fingertip into the hollow of her navel, sealing an umbilical connection. He felt a sensation of oneness, of having touched together before.

"*Kamae.*" His lips brushed over the small dark mole on the cusp of her hip. The urge to kiss his way down was strong and deep and compelling. He wrestled with his grinding need, pitting it against his sense of honor and a silent vow to protect this woman entrusted into his keep.

The struggle was fierce, but in the end he managed to protect her from himself. Exhausted as much from the internal clash as the physical rigors that surviving the ocean had demanded, he laid his head against her heart and drew her into his arms.

He needed rest and escape from the urgent male drive to possess her unconscious body. Sterling fell into a light sleep, comforted by the feel of her breast cushioning his face, his hand in her hair, and the sweet connection of fingertip to navel.

Two

She supposed she was asleep and having a strange dream in which she could feel the bed beneath her back. But somehow she knew she was straddled between sleep and consciousness. Was she in the motel room, sleeping off the complimentary champagne?

She stretched slightly, feeling oh, so wonderful. She didn't really want to wake up. Especially not when the mattress was so comfortable, and the air was balmy and smelled of salt water. She must have left her balcony door open and a breeze off the ocean was sailing in. . . .

A wisp of air brushed across her skin and circled her waist. Then she felt something moist dip into her navel. The sensation was totally unexpected and wildly exciting. It made her belly coil tightly and her hips rise as a low moan settled in her throat.

This dream was amazingly real *and* too good for her to want to wake up. Surely, she hadn't invited one of the men who'd flirted with her at the bar into her room? Even if she was pretending to be someone far more exciting than she really was, the timid mouse inside her would never have permitted such an uninhibited, risqué thing to actually happen. Ingrained with traits she resented but couldn't shake, only in her dreams could she chuck it all and cut loose without a care about her reputation or tomorrow.

The pressure increased, and she could feel something akin to breaths lightly fanning over her breast. Her nipples grew achy and taut. No, she definitely did *not* want this dream to end. If she had invited a man to her room, she would make it last as long as possible before reality and good sense intruded.

She could feel herself arching, her breasts yearning, demanding more. A welcome warmth covered her, causing the strangest sensation. Her muscles seemed weighted, lethargic as if in a deep sleep, and yet they were becoming acutely sensitized. She hurt with the awakening need.

There was a feathering between her thighs, and she parted them, eager for a more vivid fantasy. The teasing wisp of sensation spread, a feeling so wonderful and rich, only a madwoman or a prude would refuse. She wasn't crazy, and uptight was reserved for the woman she'd left behind the library desk.

The pace was slow, the pressure not enough, and she tried to move closer to ease the building tension. Her hips were rocking and rising from the bed. Her breast seemed moist but insulated by warmth, as though she was being mouthed and caressed in a most careful, intimate way.

She thought she whispered, "More."

Something that might have been a hoarse groan vibrated against the tender flesh of her breast. Fingertips fanned her open, grazing over her moist heat in tiny circles while a palm clamped over her mound and pressed.

Her fingers dug into the softness beneath her, and an anguished cry of need tore from her throat as she thrust up to fill the empty hurt.

Her loud moan echoed between her ears.

Her mind snapped from fantasy to awareness. Diedre suddenly realized she was on the ground and someone was in the act of pressing a finger intimately into her body.

"Oh my God!" she cried, causing that someone to jerk with the sudden, shrill sound of her alarm.

She watched in disbelief as the man's head slowly, hesitantly lifted from her breast. He shifted until his mouth nearly touched hers. Though his face was cast in shadows, she saw its dark intensity, its familiar features etched with a primitive passion. He blinked several times, as though struggling against the remnants of sleep and the throes of a hot, sensual haze. His eyes mirrored the wild and furious instinct that was taking her over and banishing her natural timidity.

She froze in mid-arch, too stunned to be completely horrified. Desperately, she tried to remember who he was while struggling against the sizzling sensations that still held her in a taut grip.

"Don't be scared," he said in the grainy voice she recognized. "I'm not going to hurt you."

Diedre nodded, afraid to move, acutely aware of his hand inside her pants. He was very still, his fingertip pressed at her point of entry.

"What are you doing?" Her voice sounded strident. She could hear her words bouncing between her ears and out to the jungle surrounding them.

"It seems I'm doing something I thought going to sleep would prevent. Looks like I was wrong."

She felt his hand depart with a single, svelte glide, only to rub over her half-bare belly in a way that might ease a stomach ache but managed to increase her confusion and distress. The man was causing an uncomfortable awareness that didn't fit into the boundaries that defined her neat, orderly world.

"Relax," he soothed. "I know it's asking a lot, but trust me. You're safe."

"Why should I trust you?" Her fingers clenched something soft, and Diedre realized she was lying on a bed of large leaves. As discreetly as possible, she scooted sideways, trying to put a little distance between her and him.

"No reason," he answered. "But even at that, I'm a safer bet than what you'll find out there."

Darting a furtive glance into the descending darkness, she was dismayed to see that he was right. Even if she could outrun him she'd be surrounded by an alien world that definitely posed a greater danger.

"I'm sorry about what happened. Well, actually I'm not, but that's no excuse for fondling you, asleep or otherwise. If you want to slug me, you're perfectly justified." He offered his cheek. "I won't hit back."

Half of her *did* want to take a punch; the other half reeled with a startling realization: The main reason she wanted to strike him was because he hadn't finished what he'd begun before she awoke.

"Who *are* you?" she demanded in a shaking voice.

"Guess I should have introduced myself earlier. The name's Sterling Jakes, though I can't blame you if you want to call me something a little more colorful."

His smile was apologetic. Her frustration and fear receded, though her sudden self-consciousness didn't. Diedre glanced down and saw her blouse gaped open, revealing her plain cotton bra. It was wet, and her nipples were puckered against the fabric in a shockingly provocative display.

Before she could cover herself, he pulled the torn shirt together with efficient movements, then patted it once. The gesture struck her as strangely reassuring, sweet in an odd way.

She struggled to sit up, surprised her body felt so

tender and bruised after what had to have been a very long rest.

"Let me help," he said, carefully easing her to a sitting position. Diedre shocked herself by accepting his assistance and not instinctively shrinking from his too familiar touch.

"Thanks," she said awkwardly, darting a wary glance at the man who was suddenly busy with his knife and a coconut. His hands worked the tool into the fruit with agility and speed, sure of whatever it was he was doing and reminding her of just how accomplished he was in handling her, even in sleep. She could only wonder what he was capable of when fully awake and applying his skills with the intention to seduce.

"Drink a little of this." He fitted the rough hull to her lips, and she forgot the utter strangeness of the situation. She was parched. The liquid streamed down her throat, and she grasped his hands, trying to gulp down the sweetness.

When he pulled away the coconut, her ingrained manners and social breeding fled in the face of instinct's demands. She nearly lunged at him, trying to grab the coconut back.

"Not too much," he said firmly. "Not until I'm sure it's staying down."

"I'm dying of thirst," she groaned. "I have to drink some more."

"You nearly died of drinking too much. The last thing you need is to make yourself sick after drowning."

"Drowning?" she repeated numbly.

"The sharks thought we were bait, and I lost my grip on you. You were unconscious, and it was touch and go. I didn't know if we'd make it to shore, and once we did you were already flirting with the angels." His mouth quirked in a semblance of a smile. "Glad you decided to stay."

She had died? Flying down a long black tunnel surrounded by brilliant light hadn't been a dream? The realization made her head swim. She fell back on her elbows and willed the dizziness to pass.

She didn't want to remember drowning. She didn't want to think about a stranger's touch setting off primal responses she couldn't possibly possess. What she did want was for this nightmare to end, for her to go home, brew a cup of Darjeeling tea, and curl up beside the fireplace with Emily Dickinson or Stephen King, or at this point, even the back of a cereal box.

The dizziness passed. Diedre stared directly at the man named Sterling, determined to face whatever facts he might provide.

"You mean you resuscitated me?"

"Mouth to mouth." His gaze gravitated to her lips and lingered. "Though usually I prefer some reciprocal participation."

She fidgeted under his scrutiny.

"You saved my life. I'm . . ." She searched for adequate words and found none. "I'm very grateful. I can't thank you enough, Mr. Jakes."

"Mr. Jakes?" he repeated with a laugh. "Considering our circumstances, you can thank me by dropping the formalities, Ms . . . ?"

"Forsythe. Diedre Forsythe."

"Diedre. Nice. Kind of goes with that cultured, ladylike voice. Reminds me of someone I know from Boston, street side, though being a betting man, I'd wager you've got more breeding than street savvy." The lines fanning from his eyes crinkled as he studied her with open curiosity. "You wouldn't be one of those blue bloods from around Hyannis Port, would you?"

When she didn't reply, he stroked his stubbled chin. "A few years back a buddy and I sailed around Nantucket Sound. Some of those mansions I saw through the binoculars—whew. Pretty impressive. I could picture you living somewhere like that."

Diedre's back stiffened. She was doing her best to put her roots behind her, but even when she was in such dire straits, the man had her placed. Her rigid spine automatically turned to jelly as a slithering, creepy-crawly noise sounded behind them through the brush. Forgetting her ire, she edged closer to Sterling and focused on him rather than whatever was rustling in the night.

"My family lives there," she admitted reluctantly. "I haven't seen them in a while. My apartment's in Fond du Lac, Wisconsin, close to my job at the local library." Quick to assert her hard-won independence, she added proudly, "I'm not rich. Actually, I'm on the financially lean side."

"A librarian?" Apparently, he was more interested in that than her money, which Diedre decided definitely stacked the chips in his favor.

"Just reference for now." Her small laugh was laced with uneasiness as the rustling came closer.

"Keep talking, but don't move." He slowly stood up, and to her amazement began to stalk the noise on feet so soundless, he could have been levitating.

"I'd like to be a head librarian one day, but reference is a good place to start." Her voice was a squeak. Even if she'd wanted to, she couldn't have budged, since paralysis had apparently set in. Only her eyes dared to follow his measured paces, while her heart lodged in her throat.

"That's the wonderful thing about working around books. A person never stops learning—"

He touched his finger to his lips, commanding her to be silent. She wanted to shut her eyes but was too terrified to do more than lock them on Sterling. What would she do if anything happened to him before they were rescued? she wondered wildly.

He jerked down with lightning speed, quicker than she could blink. His motions were smooth, precise, the fluid actions of a piston-driven human machine. Just as quickly, the slithering noise stopped, and he snapped back up with a long, slender object. His arm was a blur as he cracked the thing like a whip. Its tail thrashed in outrage, and Diedre saw that Sterling Jakes held the serpent's gaping jaws open with his thumb and forefinger.

Diedre's shriek died on a strangled gasp when he sliced off the head. It fell to the ground and rolled to her feet. She scrambled to get away from the forked tongue flickering near her heels and the sightless glassy eyes staring at her with venomous hostility.

He threw the rest of the reptile close to its head, and in morbid fascination Diedre watched the dismembered body continue to twitch and squirm.

She lifted her head; it felt jerky, as if in need of some oil where it connected with her neck.

She stared at him in disbelief. "You killed that snake."

"Uh-huh," he said, preoccupied with swiping the knife across his jeans, then inspecting the blade for residue. Finding none, he sheathed it. "Never did like slimy stuff left on my knives. Good way to start some rust."

"What are you going to do with that horrid thing?"

"Hungry?" He cocked his head and grinned. "Once its body gets the message, I'll skin it and make us some supper."

"Supper?" she repeated incredulously. "You don't actually expect us to eat a snake?"

"Got any better ideas? It's getting too dark to go fishin'. Besides . . ." He closed the distance between them with a few long strides. "The meat's good, and we need to eat for strength. You more than me."

She stared up at him, realizing for the first time

how much taller and larger he was. He smiled en-
couragingly while his hand—so strong and large it
was capable of annihilating a snake—came to rest on
her shoulder, then slid up and down on her upper
arm.

His eyes held a hint of humor, but also of remembered intimacy. She lowered her gaze, and it fell on
the serpent's lifeless form.

"You've eaten one of these?"

"Lots. Rattlers, pythons, and other assorted varie-
ties. Green Berets have a nickname—Snake Eaters.
Tasty critters, snakes. Even without salt."

She slowly met his eyes, and the gaze that locked
with hers jolted her senseless. *What kind of man
was Sterling Jakes?*

He wasn't a college fraternity brother trying to cop
a feel at a party. Neither was he the conservative,
steady type she'd leaned toward since she'd earned
her degree. Best of all, he was anything *but* one of the
high-society pedigrees her parents had been pushing
down her throat for years.

"I suppose I could try it," she ventured bravely.
"After all, you did save my life. That tells me I should
trust you on this."

"Good girl." He patted her back with affectionate
approval, but his hand lingered with a parting caress.

"Tell me what to do."

"You just watch this time. It's very important you
learn some basic skills, in case something happens
to me."

"But why? We're both safe now, and surely we'll be
found soon. Don't you think a search was started
when we didn't make it back? Rescue's probably on
its way this very minute."

Sterling's heavy brows drew close together, but his
expression gave nothing away. She was disturbed

when he simply said in a low voice, "While you were napping, I put together a rough SOS on the beach. I also piled up some dry wood and brush. We'll start a fire, since you're getting cold."

Diedre realized she was shivering, though it was a warm, sultry night. She did feel chilled—from shock, from her body's belated reaction to trauma. But most of all from the tingle racing up her spine and prickling the fine hairs on her neck.

Tilting up her chin with the crook of his finger, he studied her face. For a few heart-tripping seconds she fully expected him to kiss her.

"I'll get the snake, and you follow me. Okay, partner?"

She felt a strange sort of melting inside, a lovely sense of companionship with this unlikely comrade who was including her in his auspicious ranks. He couldn't know it, but he'd just given her something she craved. It was a feeling of belonging that only her books provided, but that vanished as soon as her nose was no longer between the pages and her eyes pried from the printed words.

She smiled with gratitude, glad that he probably assumed it was for his earlier heroics.

"Lead the way . . . partner."

He gave her a wink, then bent down and swiped up the snake. Swinging its tail like a lasso with one hand, he clasped hers in the other.

"Forward and to the beach, me matey. Time to sing around the campfire and roast the longest hot dog you ever ate in the uncivilized world. Unfortunately, I left the marshmallows at home."

"Then I don't suppose you remembered to bring the jam box with the Beach Boys tape along, either?"

His sudden burst of deep laughter startled her, and from the noises erupting from the jungle, apparently some other life forms she didn't care to consider.

Surefooted, he forged ahead, seemingly with X-ray vision. Diedre couldn't see more than two feet in front of her, but as long as she held tight and kept her eyes on Sterling, she felt safe, protected.

Three

Sterling was mutilating the second Beach Boys' song even worse than the first when Diedre dissolved into a giggle.

"Hey! What're you laughing at?" Sterling looked up from the spit he was turning on two Y-shaped branches.

Diedre immediately fell silent, but the indignant glare he shot her from the opposite side of the small fire set loose the giggle about to strangle her throat. It slipped past the dam of politeness and burst loudly from her lips.

"I'm . . . I'm sorry," she finally managed to say, wiping a tear of mirth. "It's just that . . . you might be able to build one heck of a fire, but the way you sing—"

"What? Don't you know talent when you hear it?" He repeated the chorus that had set her off, more off-key than before, if that was possible.

"Yes!" Diedre couldn't help howling with laughter. "I'm sorry to be untactful, but your singing reminds me of one of those hound dogs baying at the moon."

"I guess that beats the person who told me I sounded like a cat in heat getting it on in the alley."

A blush stole into Diedre's sunburned cheeks. She fleetingly wondered how her mother would react to such an indelicate analogy. A vision of her eyes popping out through her opera glasses made Diedre laugh all the more.

"You're starting to look pinker," he noted. "Want me to put some more *Aloë vera* on for you?"

Diedre considered his offer. She wasn't sure if she could endure another treatment. The plant's juices had been very soothing, but sitting there motionless while he smoothed the thick, sticky substance over her face and neck and arms had set her on a nerve-wracking edge.

"Not yet," she decided, while her feminine urges promptly sighed in disappointment. "Maybe we should try something besides the Beach Boys."

"Heard any good arias lately?" he said, laughing. "How about something from *Madame Butterfly*?"

"Sure," she agreed, and launched into a lilting cadence of much practiced, scaling notes. She let them flow through her, enjoying the freedom of her voice soaring into the heavens. Here, there were no rigid expectations, no need to measure up.

The music peaked, and she just missed a high, demanding note. Automatically, she stopped.

"Go on. Please."

There was a timber of awe in his low voice. She was surprised to see that he was staring at her with the admiration her peers had reserved for those more gifted than she.

"I got carried away, I guess." Diedre coughed, flattered but slightly embarrassed. "My throat's still a bit raw, so I think I'd best quit."

"You're good," he stated. "Better than good. Why weren't you in an opera house instead of working behind the stacks?"

"I can carry a tune, but I don't quite cut it on a professional level." She shrugged, all too aware of her vocal shortcomings. The joy had been lost years ago—and she hadn't recovered it until just now. "Besides, the library is where *I* want to be. I love books. I couldn't live without them."

His heavy brows drew together, and his features settled into an expression she couldn't decipher. He seemed ready to say something, but instead he assumed that too-still posture she found both soothing and disquieting.

A breeze off the ocean wisped across the fire, causing a spark to leap out and die on the sand. The burning embers were a tepee of sticks enclosed by three large rocks laid out in a triangle.

"Remember what I said about always lighting a fire from the windy side." Sterling nodded in the direction of the escaped ash. "Since you're tired of singing, we'll pass the time with questions and answers."

"What's your favorite hobby?" she asked.

His wicked smile knocked her for a loop. "That's a personal matter you're probably better off not pursuing. For now let's stick to something a lot less enjoyable but more crucial to survival. Tell me how you'd handle my knife and the flint to get a spark and make a fire."

The spark was definitely there, she thought, and the man had real talent when it came to making more than one kind of fire, which apparently included his favorite hobby.

"First you start with the punk," she said, warming as she remembered his deft handling of the simple tools, his easy, patient manner of instruction.

"And where do you get the punk?"

"Find some small pieces of rotten wood, dry enough to crumble."

"Next?"

"A piece of cloth. Rip a little piece of material off your clothes."

"Right. And by the way, thanks for the loan."

˙ He glanced down the front of her shirt. She could still feel the tug of his hands on the ragged tail of her blouse; she could still hear the jagged ripping sound while he sliced through the fabric. It had been necessary, but to her civilized mind there had been a savageness in the action, something a little barbaric and strangely thrilling. Especially with his massive bare chest all but touching hers.

Hurtling her usual shyness, Diedre stole a furtive glance at his chest now. Whatever form of exercise he employed must greatly emphasize his upper body. Whenever he tensed, the muscles assumed the shape of hard blocks. When he relaxed, she was reminded of a great stallion after running a hard race, with muscles rippling beneath his dark skin. Despite his oversized build, he was more lithe than heavy. Even with the generous swirl of hair covering his chest, she'd spied several ominous-looking scars that some-how only enhanced his disturbing appeal.

Realizing her glance had lengthened into an out-right stare, she shifted it to his face. His gaze held a naked intensity that was jarring, as bare as his chest; it was the look she imagined a man might wear in the pinnacle of labored passion.

Stunned by the direction of her thoughts, Diedre quickly looked away.

"What do we do once we run out of . . . clothes?" It was a practical question, but she had to force herself to allude to their potential nakedness. "That's a silly question," she said quickly. "We'll be long gone from here before we have to resort to wearing fig leaves."

No comment came from his corner. She felt his focused gaze on her until she began to feel stripped already.

"Okay," he said slowly, "you've got the tinder, the fabric, the knife, and flint. Now what?"

"You make the fire." She hugged her arms tightly

around her crossed legs, shifting her attention to his steady rotation of the snake on the spit.

"Not good enough. C'mon, Diedre, I want to know how quick you can learn. What have I got here? An average student or Harvard material?"

"Brown," she answered automatically. "Phi Beta Kappa." The spit stopped turning, and she wished she'd kept the information to herself. She would have liked to be more anonymous to him, to be thought of as a simple sea waif under the stars—with this master warrior of the land for a companion.

"Hold the fabric in your hand on top of the flint," she said. "Strike the blade against the flint so that the spark lands on the material, then blow gently until it can catch the tinder."

"A-plus, darlin'. You passed the test."

Diedre smiled, pleased by his approval. "Why do you carry flint around? That's not the sort of thing most people keep in their pockets."

"It's no ordinary flint. Come over here, and I'll show you."

There was a push-pull inside her. His effect on her was almost overwhelming, and she found it took some effort to force herself up. Moving on limbs that seemed disjointed, she was aware of a heightening of her senses, so that she felt each grain of sand that worked up between her toes.

She stopped beside him. Sterling's head was tilted up toward her, the fire casting him in lapping shadows of mystery. His eyes reminded her of a kaleidoscope, its multicolored designs changing with each turn of thought and emotion. A woman could get caught in those dark, telling chambers and never want to escape.

The eyes in question traced an incisive path, beginning at her head and ending with her feet.

"I like what I see, Diedre," he said simply. He

passed his hand over the sand as if clearing a seat. "Sit with me."

She felt a little breathless, woozy, almost high. Her inner thighs quivered. Diedre dropped to her knees before her legs gave way.

With great solemnity Sterling withdrew the flint from his pocket. He held the small piece in his open palm. She looked at him in question, but he seemed to be focused inward. Was he meditating, praying?

He leaned slightly forward then, in a short, formal bow. The cryptic ritual complete, he offered the object for Diedre's inspection.

"Notice anything different?"

No, she wanted to say, *just that you're the strangest, most compelling man I've ever met outside of a book, and I'm starting to hope that search party takes its time.*

"It's shaped like a four-sided star." The heavy metal felt warm in her hand, and she thought it must still carry his heat. She tested one point with the tip of a finger. "It's so sharp. Like the tip of a knife."

"It can kill."

She glanced up in astonishment, unable to miss the significant edge he'd given to the last word.

"Has it?" she asked hesitantly, not sure if she wanted to know.

"Yes."

"A snake?"

He didn't answer.

Diedre looked from him to the deceptively benign flint. This thing in her hand had apparently taken the life of a human, though she couldn't imagine Sterling being capable of murder. The metal suddenly had a dangerous, cold feel she didn't like, one that caused her to shudder.

"But it's more than a weapon," he hastened to explain. "The *manji shuriken* star blade helps the ninja find his way to spiritual enlightenment."

"The ninja?" she repeated. The only ninja she'd ever seen were animated, mutated, and green. "I guess that means you're into karate."

"Something like that." Sterling chuckled as he brushed her palm with his fingers and retrieved his prized possession. He made another short bow before sliding it back in place.

"Is that how you can move so fast? When you grabbed the snake, all I saw was a blur. It was . . . incredible."

"The ninja have their secrets. Theirs is a very old discipline and philosophy, even a way of life. Though I'm something of an adopted black sheep, I hold to many of their teachings. Unfortunately, not all their teachings accommodate some of my fonder vices."

He leaned forward and tore off a sizzling piece of their dinner, oblivious to a flame that lapped at his skin.

"Are you hurt?" she asked anxiously.

"Hurt?"

"I saw you get burned."

Sterling shrugged, unconcerned. "The ninja—and the Berets—are good at instilling certain lessons. As the military will tell you, it's all mind over matter. The ninja are more poetic. To endure *kuro*—suffering—is good. They believe suffering gives you strength and leads to spiritual power."

"You mean what doesn't kill you only makes you stronger?"

"Bingo." Sterling took a small bite of the meat, then pronounced it done.

"However did you manage to get involved with the Western military and Eastern culture?" Not only was she more than a little curious, she wanted to avoid the "food" he was serving.

"Let's just say one sort of led to the other. We can swap life stories some day. Should make for a good way to pass the time." When she shrank back from the main course, he moved in closer and teased her lips with it. "C'mon, darlin'. It's chow time."

"I've decided I'm not hungry." Diedre kept her lips pressed together although the hungry growl of her stomach grumbled in disagreement.

"I washed my hands," he murmured seductively. "I promise they're clean. And probably a little salty. Just enough flavor to enhance this tempting, delectable treat. Though after staring at that luscious mouth of yours half the night, I'm sure it's got nothing on you."

His lips curved into a slow, lazy smile and inched perilously close to hers while his fingertips grazed over her throat.

It was a sexy maneuver from a man who was definitely seasoned, she thought. Her lips unlocked, eager to accept what was surely destined to be the most exotic, fire-breathing kiss of her existence.

Sterling cupped her chin, his fingers stroking, then closing tight. He opened her mouth with a firm clamp at her jaw. His head dipped, and she closed her eyes, inhaling the scent of smoke. Then she felt a moistness when the tip of his tongue traced her lips, only to dart provocatively inside, and with a swirling mastery probe the tender interior of her lower lip. It quivered, she felt her pulse against his tongue.

"Delicious," he whispered. "Definitely first-rate."

He replaced his tongue with his finger, the roughened pad tracing an erotic groove. He did taste pleasant, of salt and hunger. And man. His prelude to a kiss far exceeded any dreams she'd ever harbored in her soul, one yearning more than ever to find its way free.

"Diedre," he murmured with a silky voice. "You've never said my name. Say it now."

"Sterling," she breathed on a sigh.

The warm, thready substance of something that tasted like chicken made its way into her mouth.

Sterling firmly pressed her jaw closed, effectively sealing in what he had just put inside.

Her eyes snapped open. His smile was pleased; his heavy-lidded gaze promised pleasures she couldn't begin to guess at.

"*Bon appétit,* darlin'," he said thickly.

Diedre cautiously considered the merits of snake to the palate. Deciding it wasn't half-bad, she began to chew.

Four

"You did a fine job getting the fire started, Diedre."
Sterling added two heavy logs to keep it going
through their second night. "I was real proud of you."

"Thank you, Sterling," she said, beaming. "I was
proud of myself. But I couldn't have picked it up so
fast if you weren't such a good teacher. That's a
special talent in itself."

"I get plenty of practice at my *dojos*. I'll have to
teach you a few techniques in the art of ninjutsu.
Just some basic kicks, punches, and throws."

Diedre looked doubtful but interested. "That could
be fun. I guess you're an instructor then?"

"In a manner of speaking. I'm a black belt, fifth
degree. My training started in the service, but my real
education came from Japan. I still have a lot to
learn." When she asked him to elaborate, he sidestepped it with a shrug. "I'll tell you more . . . one of
these days."

She missed the implication of time and gave a low
whistle. "Wow. An authentic fifth-degree black belt. I
wouldn't want to tangle with you."

"Sure about that?" He let a hint of insinuation

flavor his smile. It grew broader with the heightened color of her cheeks, the bashful dip of her head.

"Know what I wish I had right now?" Diedre was suddenly busy examining the chipped polish on her nails.

"A manicure?"

"No." She giggled. "Dental floss. It's one of my darkest secrets."

"Got a thing for it, huh?" He caught her hands and examined them. They were pampered, he thought, but not for long. They were also moist with sweat, a giveaway that the attraction between them was mutual. He rubbed them, spreading the moisture under his thumb. "Have you got a cache of it stashed at home?"

"No, just a few containers. I prefer the waxed, mint-flavored kind. Like American Express, I don't leave home without it. Whenever I go out to eat, I always sneak into the ladies' room during the meal because I can't stand to have anything between my teeth. It's one of my quirks." She darted him an anxious glance at the same time he felt the tremor of her hands. "Promise you won't tell anyone?"

"I give you my word," he said solemnly. The urge to laugh was squelched by the growing likelihood there would never be anyone else to tell. Releasing her hands, he set about laying out a pallet of palm leaves. "I'll look for some beeswax tomorrow. You can chew it in lieu of brushing."

"If it's too much trouble, I can wait till I get back to the hotel. Surely, we'll be back by this time tomorrow. Actually, I'd expected to see our rescue party today."

Sterling contemplated his answer. She'd already been through too much. He didn't think she was ready to know about the small craft he'd heard in the distance a few hours after daybreak. They hadn't been spotted, and neither had the crude SOS sign he'd made out of fallen limbs. His expert knowledge of the area told him that was due either to the absence of wreckage the search party was looking for, or to the Triangle playing one of its infamous tricks.

People had been known to see planes overhead, but for some strange reason island occupants and structures were rendered invisible from the air. A trick of lighting? An atmospheric anomaly? Or maybe some unseen force that defied the rational mind of man? He was inclined to believe there was a scientific explanation. Then again, considering what he knew about the Triangle, he was just superstitious enough not to rule out an implausible cause.

"We'll see," he finally said. Quick to get off the subject, he finished making their bed. "Know what I wish I had right now?"

"A sheet?"

"A beer. No, make that a six-pack with a bottle of sake on the side. I could use a cigarette too." He stretched out on his back. "Lie down with me, and we'll go to sleep looking at the stars."

"Together?" Her gaze skittered over the single bed. He'd made two pallets the night before.

He extended his arm, indicating where he wanted her to be. It was impossible to miss the awkwardness of her movements when she hesitantly obliged, or the way she stiffened when he pulled her against his side. Until now he'd been careful to keep temptation to a minimum. This probably wasn't wise, but he needed the comfort that feeling her next to him gave. She fitted well, her shoulder tucked under his, her curves a soft, inviting contrast to the hardness of his strength. It was a battle of will not to hug her tightly and give himself over to the desire that was bucking against his good intentions and threatening to take the lead.

For a few minutes they lay together in silence and stared heavenward. Without city lights the stars were brilliant, the universe spread out in display.

"Jakes-san, when will you learn? Earth, wind, fire, void. You move like wind, breathing fire. But your feet are sealed to the earth, so you only stare up at the void. Let go, Jakes-san. Flow. From the stars you see how wrong you stand."

"I see the Little Dipper." Diedre pointed to the small constellation. "The Big Dipper too. They look different from here."

"I wonder how they see us," he wondered aloud. "Maybe we look different to them too."

"I hope so," she whispered, turning and moving closer to his chest. Sterling tightened his arm, securing a natural hold.

"They could tell us something about the way we see ourselves. At least, so I've been told."

"How do you see yourself, Sterling?"

"Always reaching, but never quite able to grasp."

"I know how that feels." She leaned over and very lightly placed her palm on his chest. Her breathing was shallow, and he could feel the anxious thread running through it. "Are you married?"

"Once. It lasted a couple of years. Didn't work out."

And what of the future? What of Ming, who waited for him now on another continent? They were both probably better off if he was here for good. He could share his doubts about his engagement with Diedre. Then again, maybe not. His old problems were possibly no longer valid and could muddy the water of this new relationship that was fresh, enticing. Dental floss, he thought with an inner chuckle. She made him feel as though he'd exhaled something stale and sucked in crystallized youth.

No, he decided, he wouldn't tell her about Ming. Not when Diedre drew him until the attraction felt close to compulsion, making him act on urges that compromised his sense of honor. *Honor.* The word didn't mesh too well with the way he'd fondled her yesterday. Maybe it was his conscience keeping his impatient hands at bay now.

"Having a marriage fail must have been difficult," she said sympathetically. "I'm sorry."

"I'm not. I learned from my mistakes." Had he? Agreeing to marry a woman for the wrong reasons, no matter how worthy, hadn't been a smart thing to do. Especially when the one he held in his arms was sending messages to his heart and wreaking havoc on his resolve to back off from an immediate, no-holds-barred course of seduction.

Diedre's hand made a small movement. She was stroking his chest, he realized, but her gesture was slight, timid. He found it endearing. He also found it nudging his libido close to a precarious, dangerous edge.

"Let's call it a night. How do you sleep? What position?" Hopefully, not on her back, he thought with an inner groan. He still felt the grip of insanity. He'd come so close to joining her body to his as she'd lain unconscious and totally at his mercy on the jungle floor.

"On my side."

"Me too. Roll over. You can use my arm for a pillow."

She obeyed without question, and he gritted his teeth, vowing to deserve her trust. But even the few safe inches he put between them nearly stripped his control.

"Sterling?"

"Hmmm?" *Hup-two-three-four. Don't get closer, that's for sure. If you do, you're gonna break. Go to sleep, forget the ache. Hup! Hup! Hup-two-three—*

"What does it mean to be a ninja?"

He wished she'd hush. The soft wisp of her voice was putting his highly disciplined mental training to one hell of a test.

"The ninja is a warrior," he said tightly. "One who seeks enlightenment and purity."

"No wonder you make me feel safe."

Sterling closed his eyes so he wouldn't see the curve of her neck, the temptation she presented in profile. In the darkness of his mind he saw it anyway. He saw how she would look naked. His feet left the ground, and for once he flowed with the stars. He saw a vision in the void, a moment in which he unveiled pleasure's secrets and she embraced them with fervor, shedding all innocence, all reserve.

"I have a warrior's heart. I do seek enlightenment." Trapped by the vision, he slowly, deliberately fanned his hand over her belly. He felt her quiver, and his body responded. Pulling her flush against him, he pressed his groin against her.

"But, Diedre," he whispered roughly, "I am impure."

The smell of something cooking wafted to Diedre's nostrils. She slowly opened her eyes to the tropical brilliance of a new day. Lowering her gaze, she saw that Sterling had his back to her and was busy in what was fast becoming their kitchen.

"Afraid I can't offer you coffee," he said. "Just some more coconut milk. After breakfast we'll go find some rainwater stores."

Stretching languorously, she was sorry to think their idyll would doubtless come to an end today.

"How did you know I was awake?"

"I sensed it. How did you sleep?"

"Great! How about you?" She was a little stiff, but she'd slept like the dead. Maybe that was from lying awake a good hour being alternately apprehensive and acutely aroused by their sleeping position.

When Sterling made no comment, she prodded, "Have you been up long?"

"Oh yeah," he said shortly. "I've been up. And not for just a little bit."

His mood struck her as odd. Ignoring the fact that he wasn't being overly talkative, she edged closer to see what his culinary talents extended to this time.

"That smells delicious. You sold me on snake. Dare I hope for wild boar?"

"Nothing that exotic." He sliced off a piece of meat. "Rabbit. Try this."

She accepted his offering without hesitation. The rabbit was good, but the fleeting taste of his fingertip before he quickly pulled back was even better. This whole adventure was proving to be more exciting than any favorite book's vivid scene.

Books. Soon she'd be back in the library, far from here. Far from this man. Her real-life fantasy would be at an end. It left a sad, sinking feeling in her heart. She would go back home not quite the same, and she craved to take with her the experience of physical bonding with Sterling. For all their striking differences, her heart insisted they were soul mates.

They didn't have much time, though, and the way he was behaving now, staring at her in some indecipherable way, then jerking his attention back to the rabbit, left her with a distinct problem. *How did a woman go about getting a man to take the initiative?* She didn't dare. Did *she*?

The old Diedre Forsythe would never have had the courage, no matter how dire her need. But the old Diedre had been gradually retreating, and in this case she could only think good riddance.

She *would* do it! She would make herself take the leap before they were gone and it was too late. The decision left her feeling victorious, excited, alive. And very scared.

"This is excellent." She kissed her fingertips. "*Primo.*" Gathering her budding courage, she gingerly peeled a piece of rabbit off the spit. Remembering how Sterling had gone about feeding her, she teased his lips with it while slowly tracing her tongue around her own.

"My turn," she murmured as seductively as she could manage, hoping he wouldn't notice that her fingers were beginning to shake.

He stared at her hard, in a most unnerving way. Then, suddenly, in a swift flash of movement, she felt his iron-tight grip on her wrist. She was too stunned to do more than stare back. His eyes turned to an ominous shade of earth mixed with steel.

Her hand was so close to his mouth, she felt his harsh, ragged breath. Diedre's breath was imprisoned in her throat, and her mind constricted to a pinpoint focus until she was aware of nothing but the scent, the feel, the frightening power, of this dangerous man.

Commanding her wrist, he slowly moved it forward. The meat disappeared in his mouth at the moment she felt the graze of his tongue. His lips closed over her fingers, and she began to breathe again, only too shallowly, too fast. He worked her fingers in and out of his mouth in a symbolic way that even with her limited experience, she couldn't possibly misinterpret.

She tried to stifle the moan in her throat, but failed. Her belly coiled up tightly; the suction of his lips pulled at her womb. She ached, and the ache found its expression in a trickling between her thighs.

"Careful, Diedre," he warned softly. "Be *very* careful before you tease me like that again. We're all alone. . . ." He nipped the tips of her fingers. "And, darlin', I like to bite."

Diedre watched from the base of the palm tree as Sterling scaled it with agile grace. He moved swiftly upward by hugging the trunk with his hands and the soles of his feet in a fluid, machinelike process that didn't stop until he reached the top.

"Bombs away!" He threw several coconuts down, making an exploding noise with each landing.

Diedre laughed. She was still a bit shaken from his unexpected aggression at breakfast, but the edge of tension had been softened by their foraging excursion—an outing he suggested when the afternoon began to wane and she expressed concern that their ship was late getting in.

They'd had a good time touring a portion of the small island he was already familiar with and she knew next to nothing about. It seemed divided into shore, jungle, and outcropping rocks. Sterling acted as guide, sweeping heavy branches out of her way with an ease and politeness that suggested they were on a date and he was holding the door.

Along the way, he pointed out wild herbs and poisonous plants. They gathered the former and respectfully left the latter alone. She plucked a juicy berry from the large, curved shell in her hands, and savored its tropical sweetness in her mouth.

"Your turn," he said, dropping to his feet with the sureness of a big jungle cat.

"What! You don't really expect me to try doing that, do you?"

"I most certainly do." He took the shell from her and put it aside. Propelling her by the arm to the tree, he instructed. "Grab on. Hug it with your thighs and slide the bottoms of your feet against the rough notches."

She stared at him, incredulous. "Get real. I am *not* climbing this tree."

"I say you are. Climb, Diedre," he barked in a drill-sergeant tone.

"We need to get back to shore," she protested. "Someone might come, and we won't hear them."

"*I'll* hear them. I'll hear them long before they can spot us."

After witnessing his other amazing abilities, she didn't doubt that was true.

"But what about—"

"Put your hands like this." He raised her arms and clamped her hands around the bark. "Now do what I said with the thighs." She glared at him, and he lifted a brow in question. "Oh, you need some help? I'll give you a lift."

"Sterling!" she yelped. "What on earth do you think you're doing?"

She clung to the tree and tried to squirm away as his hands arranged themselves under her buttocks. He gave her an upward push.

"Climb!" he ordered.

"I'm climbing!" she yelled back. "All right? I'm climbing already!"

She pressed the soles of her feet against the roughened trunk, trying to imitate his monkeylike scale. She moved three, maybe four, feet, then lost her grip. Sliding down, she felt the stinging brush against her palms and cheek, the friction abrading her tender skin.

"See?" she charged, leaning her forehead in frustration against the trunk she still hugged. "See? I told you I couldn't climb the tree. But you made me do it anyway." She wiped away an unwanted tear. "And now my sunburn hurts again. It's all your fault, Sterling Jakes. That was a mean thing for you to make me do. And probably just so you could get a laugh watching me make a fool out of myself."

She sniffled, and then she felt his hands pull back her hair. His lips brushed over her cheek.

"Diedre, listen to me. I'm trying to teach you how to survive."

"Why?" she demanded. "You keep telling me that. But I don't need to know how to climb a tree or skin—" She nearly gagged, remembering his demon-stration on a rabbit they'd had for lunch. "I can drive to the store if I want fresh meat, and juice out of a can suits me fine."

"But we don't have that luxury here." He held her waist and leaned close. She wanted to arch back, to make contact, but refrained. "We can go back to camp and put on more *Aloë vera.* I'm sorry you got hurt."

"Quit changing the subject for once." She tried not to notice the way the heat from their bodies mingled. They were generating some kind of energy that felt like scalding wine flushing through her veins at warp speed. "You keep making these noises about learning this, learning that," she said, beginning to feel short of breath. "Then, every time I mention leaving, you get this closed look on your face or find something to be busy with. Why, Sterling? *Why?*"

"Because," he said softly, "I don't think anyone will find us."

Five

She stiffened, her spine straightening like a brittle rod. She made instant contact with Sterling.

"If this is your idea of a joke, I'm not laughing."

"You'll notice, neither am I." His hands slid from her waist and curved to embrace her upper thighs, pulling her behind against him. "I promise to take good care of you."

Diedre blinked, trying to get her eyes to focus. The jungle seemed to be zooming in and out, and she faintly wondered if she was battling shock on top of a hormonal overdose. Nothing seemed real; nothing except the feel of him pressing insistently against her backside. His hands began soothing a path over her thighs, while his unshaven chin grazed the top of her head. The prickle of beard against scalp created a unique sensation of pleasure and tension.

She thought that he shouldn't be doing this after what he'd just told her, that he should be raving and upset. *She* should be raving and upset. But the liquid sensations were distracting her, keeping her from losing her grip.

"Tell me why you think we'll never be rescued," she

asked in a shaking voice. Then she felt her hands being lifted and placed high on the tree.

"Grab it," he urged. "*Tight.*"

She latched on, aware of its bristled texture, aware of an erotic charge. Her breasts, parted by the trunk, were rubbing against the bark. He slid his palms down her arms, back and forth so lightly she might have thought it was the wind. Then, with thumb and forefinger, he drew down her eyelids.

"Close your eyes, Diedre. I want you to listen with your senses. Feel the tree, feel it with your body, smell it. *Be* it. Don't think with your mind, think with your senses."

She felt him straddle his thighs over hers as though they rode double on a great stick horse.

"Why are you doing this?" she whispered. It was thrilling, mind-altering, bizarre.

"Several reasons. Though I admit the way I'm going about it isn't standard procedure." He pressed closer to her, and she clutched the tree tighter, her arousal becoming so acute, she almost sobbed. "Starting this minute, Diedre, you begin to think a new way. It's essential. Until you do, I'm your commandant. You must act on command without question, until it becomes a reflex and we think, act, and work as a single unit."

"But this position—"

"Is it uncomfortable?"

"No."

"Arousing."

"Yes," she whispered, smelling the tree's nutty scent, hearing his voice blend with the trilling whistle of a bird and the rustle of leaves.

"What you're experiencing feels very good. The tree feels good, solid. It's old, calm, and sharing that with you. Just as I'm sharing myself with you. We are one with the forest, and we are one with each other. Do you understand?"

"Yes." His soothing voice had a hypnotic effect. She absorbed her surroundings; she let the sensations they generated flow through her and between her and Sterling.

"While I talk, you will remember this—your mind is strong and can withstand what I am about to tell you." He began to massage her back with firm, relaxing strokes. She sighed his name and felt his thighs grip hers tighter.

"I come from a military family. On December fifth, 1945, long before I was born, my grandfather disappeared while flying over this area on Flight Nineteen. He was a crew member of one of the five World War Two torpedo bombers that vanished without a trace, just after the war. Do you know the story?"

"I've read about . . . about the strange messages. Disoriented pilots, all their compasses going crazy. And . . . and then they disappeared from the radar. Fascinating." She arched her back in feline fashion, the massage taking precedence over whatever news he might impart. "That's why I took the cruise. Curiosity. Mmm . . . Sterling, a little more to the right?"

He murmured a low, pleased growl, then proceeded with his revelation. "Since I was old enough to read, I consumed every book ever written on the subject or about this area. Like my dad, I joined up at eighteen and managed to access more classified information as I gained rank. Except for when I was overseas, not a year passed that I didn't take time off to investigate this area by way of boat or plane. Big place. I still haven't seen it all. . . . Damn, Diedre, do you have to feel so good?"

He had relaxed her enough for her to be a little reckless. "How good do I feel?" she whispered, forgetting his earlier warning and seeking a snugger fit.

"Diedre," he groaned. "I . . . *be still*," he ordered, his hands forgetting their soothing task and clamping her undulating hips to make them stop. His voice became more purposeful and firm than spellbinding.

"The Triangle runs from the Bermuda Islands south to Puerto Rico and west to Miami. Say about forty-four-thousand square miles. Since 1945 over a hundred planes and ships, and more than a thousand people, have been lost."

"Planes and ships are lost all over the world."

"I don't exactly mean lost, more like vanished. And not leaving debris, an oil slick—something to mark the site. That's what the Coast Guard or anyone looking for us is trying to find. But what goes down here, goes down without a trace. The reason is a source for a lot of debate."

"But a fire, the sign you made—"

"It's the best we can do, but . . . honestly, there's a chance that anyone happening this way may not be able to see it. We're just a dot floating in the middle of nowhere, and trying to find us is a crapshoot. Make it more like winning the Florida lottery. Every year, in the Triangle, people disappear and are never seen again. We can probably chalk ourselves up as just another statistic."

"But we'll be missed." She was alarmed, no longer calm or as one with the sage old tree. "Surely, they'll keep looking until we turn up. Even my parents would try to find me."

"Private planes and boats can't possibly compete with the vastness of water and unpopulated islands. The Coast Guard stays busier here than in any other port. They'll look, Diedre, but not for long. And don't forget, the captain didn't get out his SOS. That makes our chances even slimmer. They have no point of reference. We vanished without a clue."

"We didn't vanish. We're here, we're—"

"Listen up. The *Martin Mariner* was a rescue plane that went in search of Flight Nineteen. They disappeared the very same way—no SOS, just static and then nothing. The next day the navy sent out over three hundred planes in the largest search ever launched. They added ships, even submarines. Hundreds of private planes, boats, yachts, joined in. Nothing washed ashore. They spent weeks looking along the Florida coast and the Bahamas for wreckage. *Wreckage*, Diedre, not survivors. Without seeing something of the boat we took, they have no reason to believe we're alive. As far as they're concerned, that means no us."

"You mean they're not looking for us?"

"What they're looking for are bodies and debris. There's simply too much area to cover, so the best we could even hope for is a cursory once-over. I didn't want to tell you this, but I think you have a right to know. I saw a small craft pass by yesterday before you were awake. They didn't sweep in very close, and they didn't bother to linger. Either we were too far away to catch their notice, or something made them unable to detect us."

She was beyond speech. Sterling's voice had been low, but chilling, although he'd told her nothing but the bare bones of a shattering revelation.

She slumped, giving the tree her weight while her fingers clenched into the wood.

"Do you think they're still looking now? I mean, there is a chance. Nothing's for certain, and—"

"Since it was a deep-sea, all-day cruise, they probably didn't get concerned until no one showed up by nightfall the day we disappeared. Once the alarm was sounded, they would have scanned the immediate area, since boats have been known to go down in sight of shore. We drifted quite a ways. I'm not even sure how far we're out, just that it's off the beaten track and somewhere between the Bahamas and Bermuda. By early yesterday all parties involved would have known what was up. It's the third day, and already close to dusk. The thrust of the search is over."

"Then we should try to make a raft," she insisted urgently, battling a rising sense of hysteria. "You can do anything, Sterling. You could make a raft, and we could—"

"Die." He wound his hand into the hair at her nape, then pulled until her head lay back on his shoulder. "You listen to me," he said sharply. "I can do a lot of things. I can live off the land and make crude tools, do whatever it takes to meet our needs. I can swim fifty miles in decent conditions. But fifty miles wouldn't get us to inhabited land. Even if it did, the sharks would get me first. Accept it, Diedre—we're marooned. Don't try to fight the stark, brutal facts."

"But you *could* make a raft?" Her voice was rising, and she could feel the tree choking beneath her paralyzing grip.

"In time I could put something together. If I were alone, I'd risk it. But I refuse to leave you stranded here by yourself, knowing chances are I'd die before finding help."

"You could take me with you—"

"So we could have double plots in a watery grave? What you're suggesting is a drastic, irrational act. *No*, Diedre. We're staying put. It was by the grace of God we got here in the first place."

For a long time she said nothing, only absorbing the total bleakness of their plight. Sterling's narrow-eyed stare was hard, uncompromising. His lips were taut, a straight, grim line. He was forcing her to accept the unacceptable.

"No books," she suddenly whispered. "No . . . hot baths. Or a comb . . . or soap . . ." He relaxed his grip, and she touched her hair. The fantasy was no longer a fantasy. The hair beneath her fingers felt stiff and gritty, and there was no rescue ship taking her to the hotel to wash it.

Repulsed, she jerked away from his hold. She whirled with a burst of adrenaline, and thrust him away. She stared at him, her eyes wild, horrified.

"You touched my hair," she accused shrilly. "How could you touch my hair? It's nasty, it's dirty, just like the rest of me."

"I think your hair's beautiful. And just for the record, I think you look sexy as hell."

"Don't tell me that! I can't stand to even touch my hair myself. Stay away from me! Don't touch me again! I feel like I'm covered with lice."

She began to swipe imaginary vermin from her arms and to tear her fingers through her unwashed hair like some skid-row bum battling DTs in the gutter. He reached for her. Diedre slapped his hands away, then raised her fist, ready to strike.

Vaguely, she realized she was behaving irrationally, madly, but she wanted to lash out, to break something. Her world, her identity, even her ingrained need for cleanliness, had just been stripped away.

He grabbed her, catching her fist before she could land the intended blow. She raised the other, but with infuriating ease he manacled both wrists with a single hand, then lifted them high, as though he might hang her from the tree.

His eyes sent warning messages; his expression was controlled but shaded with frustration, the hint of brewing anger edging dangerously close to stark desire.

"I will find a place for you to bathe," he enunciated carefully. "I will make what you need to wash your hair. I'll even be happy to wash it for you."

"The hell you will," she spit, grappling for lost control. "Who are you to tell *me* what you'll do—some barbarian who thinks he's the law of the land?"

"The land makes its own laws, and we will bend to its rule. There is no civilization for us, only a hierarchy based on survival. The strongest leads. Until you're ready, that role falls to me."

"I suppose that makes you king around here, and I'm your humble subject?" She wished she were the stronger. If she were, she wouldn't hesitate to hit him now. She wanted to hit him until he relented and took them from this nightmarish place, to a reality where she belonged.

"What I'm telling you is this—we assume our necessary roles. I am the protector, the provider, the teacher. You do what our necessities dictate, and you learn. There are unseen dangers you don't understand yet, but I'll see to it that you do. If I'm sick or hurt, my responsibilities fall on you. This is how we survive."

"You sound like a savage who's right at home. Get your filthy hands off me, you despicable—" He leaned closer. His free hand fanned over her behind, and he ground her against the evidence of his lust. Her instinct for self-preservation told her to choose her next words carefully. "You're a beast."

"Not yet," he said between clenched teeth. "But rest assured, we'll both begin to lose our civilized manners, as if we haven't already. The process might be slow, but we'll change, Diedre. The way we eat. The way we think. The way we speak, act, and dress." He suddenly released her arms and grasped her jaw in one huge hand. His face loomed large, bearing down on hers.

The way we mate.

She tried to shake her head, disbelieving this was happening. Disbelieving she could already feel something wild, inhuman, unfolding inside herself.

"Have you ever been kissed by a savage?" he demanded.

"Stop it," she hissed, impotently thrusting her fists against his chest. "I won't let you do this."

"Spit in the wind, Diedre. Savages don't ask for permission."

She opened her mouth to scream a hateful epithet, but he pressed his lips over hers and the sound of her fury only echoed in the chamber of his mouth. He had the good sense to keep his tongue to himself, otherwise she would have bitten it. He settled for a hard, masterful kiss. His lips crushed hers, rubbing this way, then that, before he sucked them, swollen and throbbing, into his mouth.

The way he took them was brutal, but the brutality cut through her madness, wooing back her rational mind. He began to nurse her lips with a softer pulling and a slow, sensual finesse. She quit fighting him—and herself—and accepted his smooth sip and tug. Somehow the balance between conquerer and conquered shifted, leaving two people with a mass of want, depraved with mutual need.

He lifted his head, and hers fell back. She heard their breaths mingling unevenly. The scents of their volatile emotions and struggle filtered through the balmy air. They looked at each other with new eyes, eyes that were slitted and saw nothing but the object of their desire.

He grazed her tender lips with his chin, and she kissed the stubbled square jaw, fitting her tongue into the dimpled cleft.

"Now I'm asking," he whispered roughly. "Kiss me."

She slid her hands up into his unbrushed hair. Their mouths met in tender fashion. She gave him her tongue, and he treated it well. Far better, she thought, than any woman surely deserved, as he played it to a rippling cascade of poignant, unspeakable pleasure. Opening her mouth, she asked him in. His tongue was a little rough, sliding under and around, far into the interior reaches. He tasted of the wild mint he had chewed earlier.

Without breaking the kiss, he walked her backward until she was supported by the tree. She felt his hand create a small friction as it moved surely and steadily between her legs. Her thighs splayed at his insistence, trembling now, and he lifted her until she fit them around his waist. The ripple of muscles threading his bare stomach caressed her feminine hollow. She experienced a deep ache, deeper than the one already holding her enthralled and prisoner to its grip.

She clenched inside; her fingers bit into his shoulders. A mournful, pleading wail found release from her throat. He answered it with a harsh, guttural groan.

She had no choice. Her tortured body was fevered, tearing her up with demands for satisfaction. Rubbing against him, she sought some means of escape from this terrible thing that had no name but was mighty and demanded her complete surrender.

He slid her down beneath his waist and ground against her. She heard them make growling noises, animal sounds, as they pumped in a frenzy against each other.

Then there was the rasping sound of her zipper as he forced it down. His hand, impatient and demanding, made its way through the opening. The stimulation that followed was too much to accept. She was drowning, sucked so far down she was under, with no time for a shuddering breath of air.

Who was she? What had happened to timid Diedre Forsythe? She had become this wild, writhing woman deep in a jungle with a man who had saved her, protected her. The same man she had lashed out at in exchange for his honesty and concern. She'd actually tried to strike him!

He was touching her, feeling her deeply, and they were both in a mindless sexual heat. It was frightening, this out-of-control desire heaped on an overload of trauma. And yet here she was, matching his push with her thrust.

"You're a virgin," he said in a thick voice. "You're too tight not to be." He wedged her hand between them, making her feel the means to their release and letting her know the pain it would bring. "God, I don't want it to be, but this time, it's your call. Just make it fast before I decide for you."

He was built there in corresponding proportion to the rest of him. What had she been doing? What had she been thinking? She must be insane, insane.

Her mouth open, she stared at him, almost wishing he hadn't given her the ultimate choice, that he hadn't pitted the two women inside herself against each other in a battle for supremacy.

"No," she finally answered in a ragged and raw voice that couldn't be hers.

"Okay." His whisper was strained. "Okay . . . not yet." He was breathing erratically; they both were. He rested his forehead against hers, and his eyes shone with a strange light that seemed to draw from some unseeable source. "But soon, Diedre. *Soon*. The urge is too strong inside me. . . . It's trying to claw its way out. The same urge is in you too. It won't be long before it takes over both of us. Nature dictates it. God made woman and man for each other."

"I want to go home," she whimpered.

"You *are* home." He zipped up her pants hastily; then, lifting her into the cradle of his arms, he began to forge an uncharted path through the jungle. She nestled her face in the crook of his neck, trying to muffle her sobs.

"Don't cry, darlin'," he said gently. "We're on our way to find you that bath."

Six

When Diedre awoke it was early, with the sun riding on the fading remnant of night. The muted light filtered over the pallet on the other side of the low fire. Empty. Sterling wasn't there. Neither was he busy cooking breakfast or deftly carving the slingshot he'd begun the night before as she'd watched.

Better to focus on his whittling than his dark, intense face, which her eyes had been repeatedly drawn to. He'd caught her looking at him twice, though she suspected he was aware of each brush of her gaze. His movements had stilled, and the air had assumed a charged magnetism teeming with the acknowledgment of what they had done. And what they had not.

She had looked away. Later they slept on separate beds.

Diedre got up, feeling cleaner than she'd felt since arriving. The small lagoon she'd bathed in after their heated encounter had been soothing, refreshing. It had helped clear her confused mental state, yet had done little to subdue the unfamiliar aching need within her. In fact, that need had intensified with the sight of Sterling's broad, tense back turned to her as he saw to her safety and the knowledge that he grappled with his own demons of gripping frustration.

Stoking the fire now, Diedre welcomed solitude, even if the absolute isolation was strange, alien. There were no city sounds, no sign of human life. Only the faint cry of birds, the gentle rush of waves at low tide. The warm, tropical breeze had the soothing effect of a hand stroking a fevered brow.

She wished for a pan. A package of bacon and a carton of eggs would be nice too. Sterling had seen to all their meals, and she'd like to surprise him with a hot breakfast. Perhaps it would make up for the slurs she'd hurled at him and wanted to take back. Too late to swallow the words, though, leaving her with just this feeling of shame.

Deciding she would apologize and put things right, Diedre looked around and found his footprints. She followed his path, stopping at the SOS he'd made from dead saplings. It seemed a blight on the purity of deserted beach. She nudged it with her toe, feeling a slight return of resentment.

"A lot of good you did us," she muttered. "Might as well add you to the fire." Turning on her heel, she fit her foot into a much larger print on the sand. It was odd, but she felt a certain closeness, a soul-bonding with the man she was trailing.

She'd gone about fifty yards when she saw him. What he was doing was poetic, powerful, riveting. It wasn't a ballet. Nor could she describe his fluid, precise motions as a familiar form of exercise. She watched, entranced.

With only the seascape as companion, he kicked sideways, pivoted, struck several times in rapid succession, then jabbed. The elaborate sequence of movements was propelled by so much concentrated strength, she could only liken it to . . . there was nothing she could liken it to.

Suddenly, he soared upward, turning in midair as though he weren't bound by gravity.

He landed in a position that suggested he was ready to take on an unseen enemy. Diedre couldn't help but think that only a madman would challenge a warrior as magnificent as he.

Then he spotted her. A slow, pleased smile curved his lips. It told her he was glad to see her, that he found her quite to his liking, definitely in more ways than one.

He wanted to be with her, and no other would do.

Diedre acknowledged his smile, matching it with a warm one of her own.

He nodded, then turned sharply to the sea and made a short bow.

"Mornin'!" he called, heading her way at a fast jog. Miraculously unwinded, he reached her before she could reply. Their gazes met and held, eyes filled with memories . . . and caution.

"You're up early. I thought I'd be back before you were awake. What happened?" he teased. "The smell of something cooking usually seems to set off your morning alarm."

Diedre hesitated. "I sensed you weren't there. I . . . missed you. So I woke up."

His smile softened. He brushed a strand of hair from her face. "I'm glad you missed me." Pressing a kiss to her forehead, he said, "Anyone ever tell you how good you look first thing in the morning?"

"No."

"Then I'm telling you. And it suits me fine knowing I'm the first."

Self-consciously, she ran her fingers through her hair. In the lagoon she'd gotten the sand out, but she'd had no brush to tame the long, wild mass. She didn't need a mirror to confirm she looked more like a jungle native than Diedre Forsythe, *ex*–reference librarian.

Sterling's gaze followed her motion. And she felt a spark of instant hunger, perhaps jealousy, as though he yearned to touch her hair but refused himself the luxury.

He quickly looked away to the cloudless horizon. "The sun's coming up," he said. "Watch it with me?"

She reached for his hand and squeezed it in answer. He pulled her to stand in front of him, resting his chin on her head. She thought she felt him press his lips to her hair and kiss her once before his arms slipped around her waist and drew her to rest against his chest.

They shared silent moments, apart from the rest of the world. She felt a peaceful sense of togetherness as they watched the dawn break. Diedre thought they were truly fortunate to witness a kind of beauty that seemed reserved just for them, a privileged duo.

"Do you know what this reminds me of?" She felt the first glimmer of the sun's heat as it shimmered brightly over the sea. "A great buttery yolk on a hot slice of sky."

His chest rumbled with a faint laugh, and his arms hugged her tighter.

"Makes you think of food, does it? For such a little thing you've got quite an appetite. I always did prefer women who ate with zest, not the ones who pick at their plates like they're counting each calorie and can't enjoy the meal."

Diedre experienced a flash of possessiveness. *What kind of women had Sterling enjoyed?* Doubtless more than a few. It came as a surprise to discover that she loathed each one, especially since she'd never loathed anyone in her life. It wasn't a very nice feeling. It left her unexpectedly glad they were marooned, and she had no competition.

"I could probably go for something served under glass," she said, thinking she wouldn't mind putting a fork to one of his old lovers.

"Goodness, Diedre. I can hear your stomach growl." He laughed and added, "As hungry as you always are, you sure you're not pregnant?"

She stiffened, and his chuckle died. The answer to his ill-conceived joke was blatantly obvious to them both.

"What were you doing when I found you?" she asked, wishing back their earlier ease.

"A *kata*. It's a set of techniques I practice every morning before you're up." He turned her in his arms and cocked a brow. "Tell you what. I'll give you your first lesson right now. Give me your hand, and I'll show you how to make a proper fist."

He folded her fingers into her palm and placed her thumb over them.

"Okay, Diedre, smack it against your open hand."

"Like this?" she asked, pretending it was one of his faceless women.

"That's quite a punch you've got, lady. But you need to keep your fist flat. Make sure all your fingers connect with the object, so you get the best impact."

Diedre followed his example. She demolished a few more unfortunates, then nodded in satisfaction. "I've got it!"

"Why, darlin', I believe you do." He moved behind her and nudged the back of her locked knees. They buckled, and he caught her before she fell.

"Hey! Why'd you do that?"

"Just demonstrating what happens if you don't keep your legs bent. We'll start with the basic position." His hands glided down her thighs, and he urged her legs a slight distance apart. "You're too stiff. Loosen up."

She did her best, but it wasn't easy the way he manipulated her body with firm, knowledgeable hands. He secured her balance by bending her knees and straightening her back. Then he stood behind her in a similar position, her posterior connecting with his groin.

Sterling went still, and his hand tightened on her arm.

"Make your fist," he instructed. His voice took on a huskier timber, and he subtly leaned closer to her. She made a fist, and he drew her arm against her side. "Keep your fist tight, thumb flat and facing the sky. Now just relax and get the feel of the way you throw a punch. Move into it, so your body carries your weight through to the target."

With a firm clamp on her wrist, he guided her in a natural glide. "That's it. In at the waist, stretch and rotate, and snap out. In . . . out. In . . . out. In . . ."

Diedre could feel her breathing begin to accelerate. Each in and out created an arousing friction between their joined torsos. His voice grew a little more ragged with each repetition.

"I . . . Sterling, I think I've got it," she said before she moaned.

He stopped. For several seconds he didn't let go but kept the seal of their contact. She thought she heard him mutter a graphic word under his breath that was undoubtedly what he wished they were doing instead of this.

He moved away, and she immediately regretted the loss. Turning to stand in front of her, he shared with her a gaze that said what neither of them dared.

He tapped a finger to his lips, as if by doing so he could keep from kissing her.

"Okay," he said after a prolonged silence. "Throw your best punch." He gestured to his bare stomach. "Hit me."

"Hit you?" she repeated. "I don't want to hit you." But she'd hit him already, or at least tried, hadn't she? Diedre was reminded of the reason she'd come looking for him. "Sterling," she said softly, remorse clearly etched on her face, "about yesterday—"

"Yesterday's gone, Diedre. Let it go. We've got today and the next. And the next."

"But I behaved abominably. Never in my whole life have I struck out like that. It's not me. I forgot who I was and let something horrible take over me. I'm sorry."

"Don't be. You shouldn't beat yourself for expressing feelings you're unfamiliar with. Rage, fear . . . desire—they're in all of us. Those are strong emotions, sometimes stronger than our rational minds."

"Even you, Sterling?"

"Especially me. Rage, fear—I've dealt with them often, and not always successfully. But, Diedre, the other . . ."

He shut his eyes and took a deep breath. "That was one thing I could always control . . . until yesterday. I all but lost it then. You made me feel something unfamiliar. Something a little frightening. I'm still coming to grips with the discovery. In all the years I've trained I've gone through a lot of tests—but yesterday's was the most jolting."

She was stunned that *she* could so completely shake *him*. Diedre's feminine ego zoomed as high as a thermometer's mercury bursting past the top.

"You're telling me that yesterday was different for you?"

"Different? I'll say. And also enlightening. I learned something new about myself, about how deep unknown territory can go. I was so blinded by it, I was ready to trade my soul. But I'm not sorry for experiencing an emotion that intense. In fact, I'm grateful."

Sterling shook his head at the memory. "It was a damn wild walk, all right. Took me down a whole new path and made me realize there's more to me than I thought. You need to do the same, Diedre. As the Grandmaster would say, you can't find true freedom until you're able to let go of old beliefs. Release what you *think* you are, and just *be*. It's how we grow."

Diedre absorbed what he was telling her. He was talking about desire, the too-strong emotions she'd thought were unacceptable. And more. Much more. There was a sensation inside her that was subtle and yet incisive enough to be almost physical. She felt like a bud that had been in winter slumber, closed tightly to ward off anything threatening or unpleasant. But she could feel that bud unfurling, opening under the gentle rays of a new and glorious sun.

"That sounds like good advice. Certainly more profound than any lesson I ever took from my boring old philosophy class."

"Afraid I can't take credit for passing along what someone else told me a long time ago. I'm still working on it myself, so maybe we can get there together."

"You're on."

Sterling nodded, pleased. Then he slapped his stomach so hard, the blow cracked the air. Diedre gasped in astonishment. If he didn't have a bellyache after that, he'd have to be made of steel.

"Hit me," he ordered. He punched his stomach again. "C'mon, Diedre. You can't hit me any harder than that. It's nothing, just a tickle."

"But I don't want to hurt you," she protested.

"If anyone gets hurt, it'll be you. So be sure to keep your fist tight, wrist frozen. Keep your hips loose, and plow one straight line from your upper arm to point of contact. Give me your best shot."

"Okay." She sighed. "You asked for it."

Diedre plowed her straight line and planted her fist in his stomach. Or at least it looked like his stomach; it felt more like a slab of concrete.

She forced herself not to grimace and looked up for signs of more damage on his end. Sterling grinned.

"Not bad." He gestured toward his chest like an

opponent egging her on. "Not bad for a girl, that is. C'mon, Diedre. You can do better than that. You're no wimp . . . or *are you*?"

Diedre took the bait. She ignored the sting of nerve ends on her knuckles and took another shot. And another.

"That's it! Show me your stuff. Oh, darlin', you're good. Real good."

Diedre stopped. Sterling was nodding his supreme approval, grinning from ear to ear.

"You're right," she said, feeling the power of a well-thrown punch. "I am good. Here, take this."

"Ooof!"

"Sterling!" she cried, deserting her position to see what she'd done. "Are you hurt?"

He shook his head, though his face took on a pained expression.

"I'm okay," he said, drawing in a deep breath. "I just wasn't expecting that one. I didn't flex. Lord, I must be getting soft. No one's gotten a punch in like that for years."

She rubbed her palm over the redness in his belly.

"Can I make it feel better?" she asked, genuinely concerned.

"Believe me, darlin', what you're doing is only making it worse."

His face was no longer pained but swiftly taking on a tortured expression she recognized from the day before. She stopped in midstroke, her hand resting just beneath his navel.

"Umm . . ." She wet her lips, unsure where they went from here. "I guess the lesson's over?"

"Either it's over or just getting started." He chuckled when she quickly withdrew her hand. "Next time we'll work on kicks, and from there we'll go to throws."

What happened next was beyond her comprehension. She felt rather than saw him move. One second she was standing, the next, she was suddenly lying flat on the sand. Sterling kneeled over her, his face a breath from hers.

"It won't be long before you can do the same to me," he said. "But then again, you've been at it since the minute you opened your eyes and knocked me off my feet."

She reached up and stroked his growing beard. His head dipped, and their lips touched. There was a connection of bodies electric, and hearts no less fused.

"I missed sleeping with you last night," she whispered.

"No more than I did. But I think for the time being it's wise. Being enlightened is one thing, being male is something else. I strive for the former. The other's a no-win contest."

"You're a good man, Sterling Jakes. I'm glad I'm with you."

He kissed her nose. "And I, Ms. Forsythe, consider myself lucky to have the likes of you." He kissed her quickly, then pulled her to her feet. "Race ya," he challenged. "Take off, and I'll wait till you're halfway. Last one there cooks breakfast."

"I can already taste it," she threw over her shoulder, already hitting a fast sprint. "But you'd better lose, or you get more fruit."

She laughed up at the flurry of high, white clouds, feeling her spirits soar. The campfire was in sight when a bulk of hard muscle and glistening sinew flashed past her.

"I'll take coconuts," he said, placing his order. "And while you're climbing, throw in a few bananas on the side."

Seven

"Here you go, Diedre. More ammo for the slingshot."
Sterling handed her the rabbit-skin pouch he'd made,
filled with marble-sized pebbles.

"More?" she groaned. "C'mon, Sterling. Give me a
break. I've been practicing all morning."

"And you'll keep practicing till you've got the hang
of it. But you're right, it's time for a rest." He plopped
down on the ledge of rock and patted the space beside
him. "Hungry? I brought berries, nuts, and worms."

"Worms! That's sick. Oh God, Sterling, put them
away, would you?"

He laughed at her grimace of distaste. Feeling
like a naughty schoolboy with a major-league crush,
he promptly set about impressing her by dangling
one from his mouth.

"Kiss me, dah-ling," he said dramatically. "We'll
share the fruits of our kingdom with the worms of
our mouths."

He leaned toward her, and she screamed.

"Get that away from me, you . . . you—"

"Savage," he supplied, finishing off the questionable delicacy. Roaring with laughter at the horrified
expression on her face, he said, "They're edible. They

don't taste like much of anything. It's just the thought that's so repulsive. Oh, and the packaging too."

"But why on earth would anyone eat a worm? Ugh! That was the most revolting thing I've ever seen in my life. And don't you dare try to kiss me again until you've washed out your mouth."

He chased the worm down with a berry, then indicated she open up while he took aim. Right on target the berry landed on her tongue, and he was reminded of just how enticing a delicacy could be.

After the meal and a little beeswax to clean his teeth, he would rinse in the lagoon, then hit his special, secret destination. Diedre was going to be thrilled when he finally took her to their new home. In the meantime she had more practicing to do while he went about his provider's—and teacher's—business.

"Worms, believe it or not, are a good form of nourishment," he explained. "They're full of protein, low in calories, and are usually kept stocked in your local terrain. Remember that, Diedre. If you're ever without food, you can keep from starving by eating worms. They're not too appetizing, but better worms than wasting away." He held out another one to her. "Try it. You don't have to chew, just swallow."

"No thanks." She shook her head adamantly. "Keep the worm. I lost my appetite with that little demonstration. I'd rather practice now than eat."

Sterling tossed the spurned appetizer over the ledge and got up. He watched Diedre as she loaded the squirrel skin attached to the two elastic bands he'd had the presence of mind to work from her hair that first day on the beach. Now, twenty days later, he was even more enthralled, as he'd watched her gradual evolvement in more than a physical way.

He noticed the healthy bronze tint of her skin. Her hair was wild, clean, and bleached by the sun; it looked gorgeous and tempting and sexy. Her clothes were showing their constant wear, but in his secret cave he was busy putting his dubious but imaginative sewing talents to work, though he'd been careful to keep that from her too.

"Target?" he asked, imagining how she might look in the somewhat skimpy outfit he had in mind, made of small tanned hides woven together by strips of snakeskin.

"First branch. Big tree. Twenty feet away."

"Go for it."

She aimed. The taut, lithe muscles of her upper arm pulled back, causing her breasts to strain against the tattered shirt. Sterling took a deep, steadying breath. It was wearing him down, trying not to respond to his awareness that constant exercise had worked a certain magic and strength on the body he coveted.

"Damn," she muttered when she'd fired and missed by several inches. "Sterling, I'll never get this right. Accept it, I'm just not a marksman. Forget the practice. I'm going for a swim."

She started to leave, but he caught her.

"No. Swim all you like later, but for now it's keep on keeping on. You can do it, Diedre. If you're going to be a survivor, you can't be a quitter."

"I'm *not* a quitter." Her shoulders squared; he could see her fine hair bristle. Ah, spunk. Not the least of her alluring attributes.

"No?" he challenged, drawing on his tried-and-true teacher's tactics, his military techniques. "Looks that way to me. You can't hit the target, so you opt for a swim." He took the slingshot from her and waved her away.

"Go on, Diedre. Time for a swim. But you can forget about dinner, because you're the host tonight. What you bag is what we get. And unless you've got the hang of spearing fish, we fast. No fruit either, 'cause the way you now scale trees would make that cheating, and too easy to suit me. If you've got what it takes, it's too easy to suit you too."

She glared at him, riled, her pride pricked.

"Give me that slingshot," she demanded. "Dinner's on me, and *you* can take the swim."

He smiled, satisfied. "If you insist." He handed her the small weapon and squelched the urge to tweak her nose, then steal a long good-bye kiss. "What do you have in mind? If it's worms, don't aim too close or you'll smush 'em, and I prefer mine all in one piece."

"Beat it, Sterling," she growled, raising her chin a notch. "You're cramping my style, and I've got dinner to plan."

He gave in to the never-ending compulsion to touch her. He pressed his lips to her forehead and threaded his fingers through her hair, while his body clamored for more. His mind rebelled with rampant images of releasing the frustrating brakes on his self-control and taking her as more than companion, staking his claim as mate.

"Do you mind?" She sighed. "You've got worms on your breath."

With a wicked chuckle he let her go. "Beat your chest and do a Tarzan yodel if you need me. I'll be here in a flash. And, remember, don't go too deep into the interior."

"Right," she muttered, filling the sling and drawing her arm back for another shot.

Sterling allowed himself the luxury of stroking her a few moments longer with his gaze, pretending they had no restrictions, and that there was no necessity to repeat unwanted lessons.

With a weighty sigh he turned and scaled down the ledge. He had gone maybe fifteen feet when he felt the distinct *pop* of a pebble hitting his backside.

With a quick about-face he pointed his finger at the obvious source.

"Diedre," he ordered. "Get yourself down here. Pronto!"

He took in her guilty expression, which as good as said, "Uh-oh, I got caught." He watched intently while she made her way down. He was somewhat amazed, certainly proud, and wholly approving of her quick mastery of the outcropping. He fought the inclination to smile broadly when she intuitively and calmly sidestepped the poison ivy and confronted him with an impudent spark igniting her clear blue eyes.

"Yes?" she said. "Did you forget something?"

He put aside his wish to grin, as well as his infinite desire, and summoned a no-nonsense terseness.

"Did you just land a stone in my butt?"

She glanced away and wet her lips. She took a deep breath, which only managed to make her breasts rise and tempt.

"I did."

"Did you miss or hit the target?"

Diedre squirmed under the onslaught of his stern, probing gaze.

"I . . . I hit what I meant to hit."

He made her squirm a little longer, just to maintain some semblance of authority. Then, unable to maintain the facade any longer, he chuckled.

"Well, hot damn. Good job, darlin'. Now get out there and hit something edible. I'm too tough for more than just tasting. Then again, if you're agreeable, we could just graze on each other and make do with that."

Her eyes went wide, and she took a protective step away. What kept holding her back? Fear? The fact that her virginity was threatened by a man who was so starved to take it, he didn't trust himself past a minimum of kisses? Or perhaps she sensed his own receding conflict. Ming still hovered in the back of his mind, and therefore between them, though she was growing so faint, sometimes he wondered if she had ever really existed. Diedre existed. They existed.

"Diedre? Dare I take your silence for assent?"

"No. No," she said quickly. "I think I'd rather stick with something more filling and a lot less dangerous."

"Hmm. Good instinctive reaction. Disappointing, but probably wise."

God, he wanted her, wanted her more with each passing day. But he had to remember, they had all the time in the world. For Diedre's sake, and for the sake of their relationship, he had to do his damndest not to rush her. Only he was constantly on the brink of storming the gates. He silently recited the litany, the litany he always called upon at times like this: *Diedre deserves only the best, and don't you forget it.* Yet the best he could give her was himself, and his passion was part of the package.

Was he falling in love? Had he finally found his perfect mate? He'd been wondering about that a lot lately. He still wasn't sure, because what they had didn't fit into any familiar groove. It was absorbing, fascinating, to try to put a finger on the compelling emotional facts.

"Sterling? Is something wrong? You're looking at me so strangely."

"Nothing," he said as she stroked her palm on his beard. "Just trying to figure out why I didn't hear the rock coming. I should have, so I could have jumped out of the way or ducked. On a mission that could cost a man his life."

Sterling shut his eyes, trying to get some needed distance from the tangled web of his mind. She was messing with his head, not to mention his heart, and that wasn't necessarily good since it seemed to dull his finely tuned senses. They were still in need of his wits.

"Yell when you get your quarry. I'll be there *tout de*

suite. I want to make sure you skin and cut right. That's all part of the process."

"I understand," she said stoically, tapping the sling uncertainly on her palm.

He felt deep compassion for her. He was reminded of himself at boot camp, hating what he was ordered to do but having no other choice if he was to make the grade. The resigned, downward tilt of her mouth beckoned him to take the burden on himself. But he couldn't. Not if she was to learn the necessary, uncompromising skills for survival, so she could make it alone if it ever came to that.

"In that case, you're on your own." He grasped her shoulders as he might a comrade in arms. "You're strong. You're capable. And, Diedre, I believe in you. Now you just have to believe in yourself."

Her eyes, soft and vulnerable, met his, and stoked his need to protect and possess.

"I can do it," she promised. And he knew she would, for herself, and for him.

"Remember. Call for me."

"Yes, *sir.*" She gave a sharp salute, and he allowed himself an affectionate smile. He followed it up with an on-target swat on her rump. Diedre gasped and fanned her hands over her behind.

"What was that for?" she demanded.

"Now we're even. Don't do that to me again. The next time you aim there, I'll see that you kiss it . . . and any surrounding injuries that might swell."

He stroked her behind while he toyed with her upper lip. Her cheeks turned pink as she seemed to debate which way to turn, wanting what he wanted, but still too afraid to take passion's irreversible path. His own need was too great. He had to confront her.

"You want it, Diedre. Take the chance."

"I can't."

"Why not?" he demanded. "I've given you time. I've kept to my own bed when it's all I can do not to crawl into yours. If you're bent on keeping us apart, I think I have a right to know your reasons."

Her expression was troubled, torn, and also needy.

"All right. What happened that day by the tree scares me. I keep seeing us, the way we behaved like animals. Somehow I feel what little civilization we're hanging on to is going to be snuffed out once we cross the line from friends to intimates."

He wished he could dispute her, but he couldn't. They were slowly assuming more primitive manners, their instincts taking rightful command. And she was right—there would be nothing civilized about their lovemaking. It would plunge them down, deep into an uncharted domain that would be as close as they might get to touching the savages within.

"You know, Diedre, every coin has a flip slide. Imagine shucking society's inhibitions and having no forbidden boundaries on what you and I could share. Letting go could turn out to be the most liberating experience of our lives. It's a rare opportunity for a man and a woman, one that would be a shame to waste." He cupped her hips and pressed his erection against her soft belly. "Aren't you even tempted?"

"Yes, I'm tempted. But, Sterling, it's more than that. It's . . . our friendship. You're the best friend I've ever had, and once we go to bed, our relationship can't help but change."

"What makes you think it wouldn't change for the better?"

"There aren't any guarantees."

"Of course there aren't any guarantees. Life's a crapshoot, Diedre. If you don't go after what you want and take the necessary risks, you might be safe, but what a sad trade-off for experience and excitement and life. We want the same thing. Risk it with me, and don't borrow problems that might never arise."

"It's still a gamble." She gently pushed her hand against his chest, separating their lower bodies. Sterling scowled, but didn't force further contact. "You could take what you want right now, and we both know there's nothing I could do about it. But without my cooperation the outcome won't be what you're looking for." She patted his chest affectionately. "Patience, Sterling. Give us a little more time. What we have now is very special, and I don't want to chance losing it yet. For now, please, just be my friend?"

"The old 'let's just be friends' line, huh? Lord, I haven't heard that one in years." He sighed, his disappointment heavy. "God, woman, you're hell on my ego, not to mention my hold on the rest."

"Are you angry with me?"

"Not exactly angry. We'll always be friends, Diedre. But you've drawn a line I've got a problem toeing. It's going to be a tug-of-war between us with a rope that's already frayed. As your friend, I'm warning you—the stakes are too high, so don't expect me to play fair."

His masculine prowess still stung from her rejection. He wanted to grip her to him, to strip them both bare and force her to accept his caresses until she realized she needed them as desperately as he needed hers. The temptation was great. He took a menacing step forward.

"Take the hint and get outta here before I forget about lessons and dinner and sleeping on separate beds."

She hesitated. He flicked open the snap of his jeans. She was sprinting to the safety of jungle, slingshot in hand, before he touched the zipper. His hungry gaze followed her ripe woman's body, and he clenched his jaw, drawing on his nearly sapped supply of stamina.

Judging from her swift retreat, he was certain that Diedre got the message. She might have gained a

short reprieve, but no amount of distance would keep
her safe from him.

"Now, let me see. Rodents, cleared out. Bats, evicted.
No signs of squatting on bigger prey's territory. Still
a little damp, but home-grown sealant's ready to mix.
Rocks for the fireplace. Birchbark, roots, and . . .
oops. Need a little resin for one humdinger of a kettle.
Last but most important, vat already made and some
stout berry vintage brewing."

Sterling stretched, laughing at his priorities. His
fingers grazed the rock ceiling, and he appreciated
the fact that he wouldn't be banging his head every
time he stood. Looking around their future living
space that he put at about twenty feet by twenty—
minus a few jagged edges—he decided it would definitely do.

"Not too big and a little on the dark side. But pretty
damn cozy. Not bad, Jakes-san, you done good." Now,
if he could just keep Diedre busy for another few
weeks and the weather held so they didn't need the
shelter, he'd have it fixed right nice. He wondered if
she realized they'd lucked out so far with only a few
drizzles and no shuddering storms.

What was that he heard? Sterling suddenly tilted
his head and leaned closer to the cavern's entry. He
waited, then shrugged, deciding it had only been the
wind.

He picked up the pelts from the animals he'd
skinned, then buried—an old Indian trick to loosen
the fur so that it rubbed off easily. He considered
which garment he should work on today. The hides
were smooth, though not as soft and supple as
Diedre's skin. He didn't know firsthand, but he
suspected that her chest was the silkiest, most pliable area of her body.

He had his knife to make the punctures, the

snakeskin strips—downright exotic—to . . . His gaze fell on a pouch attached to a couple of the strips, forming a sort of G-string. Sterling tapped his lips, remembering he'd notched day twenty on his calendar tree.

The faint sound again. Sterling frowned. Tossing down the pelts, he pocketed his knife and strode quickly to the mouth of the cave. He strained, listening, trying to identify the source, the direction of the noise.

It came again.

"Diedre!" he shouted. Sterling took off, bolting to the north.

"Diedre!" he called, his heart pounding harder than his legs. He stopped just long enough to catch what sounded like a frightened, urgent yell. Pivoting to the right, he was heedless of brush and rocks, and a low-slung branch that slapped his face.

Oh God, Oh God, let her be all right. She's mine, I can't bear it if she's hurt.

He saw her then, bent over and crying, screaming his name. Breathing raggedly, he rushed to her, forcing himself not to grab her to him and hurt her worse if she was wounded.

"I'm here, darlin'. I'm here. Baby, tell me what's wrong. Tell me—"

"I . . . I—" She lifted her tear-streaked face, and he cradled it with shaking hands.

"Take a deep breath," he said, quickly scanning her face, her body, for signs of injury. "Let it out . . . and again."

She nodded when she managed some control, then gripped his wrists tight.

"Sterling, it was awful. I missed the first time. Then I reloaded and missed it again."

"It? Did something big come at you? Lord, I didn't see signs of big game, and the island's small. I never would have left you alone if—"

"No, not that. I chased it down and I—I hit it in the head."

She's okay, she's okay, he thought with an out-pouring of relief.

"What did you hit in the head?"

"The rabbit." She sniffled. "I shot the rabbit."

For a full minute he stared at her. He wasn't sure which was the stronger urge—to strangle her or kiss her senseless. He did neither, and settled for lapping up the last stray tear.

"It's always hard to kill something. But the first time's the worst."

"I didn't kill it, Sterling. It's wounded. The poor thing's suffering, and I'm to blame."

"Shhh . . . it's okay. Show me the rabbit, Diedre."

She nodded and led him by the hand to a spot several feet away. The small, furry animal was convulsing on a thicket of tall grass.

"Here." Her voice caught. "I can't stand to look, to see it in such pain."

Sterling steeled himself against the need to protect her from this. Diedre had to learn, and this was a hard lesson he had no choice but to teach. He took out his knife and placed it firmly in her palm.

"Put it out of its misery, Diedre. We can't leave it like this, and we have to eat."

"No, Sterling," she beseeched him. "Please—"

"Do it."

She leaned down, crying. His heart hurt as he watched her gently stroke the animal and beg its forgiveness. He could see her hands were trembling when she pulled out the longest of several blades from the Swiss Army knife.

She looked up with a silent plea. Mustering whatever hardness he could, he shook his head.

"Through the jugular. Quick and clean."

With an agonized sob she plunged the knife and made a precise slice. And then it was over.

Diedre slumped over the dead rabbit. She was staring at the blood on her hands and whimpering with such sorrow, she might have just witnessed the death of a loved one.

He stroked her head.

"Come here," he whispered, reaching down to draw her into his arms. He hugged her close, and she clung to his waist. She was silent, but he could feel her tears fall down his bare chest.

"I feel like a murderer," she said, sobbing. "A horrible, cold-blooded murderer."

"Don't. You acted responsibly, and you were very brave. We'll treat the animal with respect, and nothing will go to waste. The fat we'll use to make soap. I'll show you how to tan the pelt, and we'll make something for you to wear in its memory."

He kissed her softly, compassionately. Taking her face in his hands, he willed her to see his pride in her show of courage.

"You did well," he said solemnly. "Because you have what it takes, we'll survive and have food tonight."

"But, Sterling, I'd rather eat worms."

A sudden realization hit him hard. He'd flirted with the possibility, but he hadn't been prepared for its full impact. It left him more breathless than when he'd charged heedlessly over rocks and skirted the edge of jungle while he'd died a thousand deaths praying for her safety.

Sterling Jakes was in love. He was head over heels in love, and Diedre Forsythe could bring him to his knees.

He closed his eyes and embraced his mate. They were bound, sealed together tight. He accepted the most enlightening discovery of his life with a heart so full, there was no room left for a shadow of doubt.

Eight

Diedre leaned against a palm tree on the sandy cove surrounding the lagoon. She knew she should be practicing her fishing techniques with the spear Sterling had fashioned out of wood and a sharp, arrow-shaped rock.

At least lancing fish was an alternative to killing another rabbit, though she'd bagged several by now. He'd made her hunt again the very next day, saying it was like getting back on a horse after a bad fall. Her second kill wasn't nearly as traumatic, and the third even less. But she still didn't like it. She never would.

Brushing her lucky rabbit's foot against her cheek, she sighed. She was learning, tutored by a master teacher. The library seemed another world away, and the woman who worked there another person entirely. Someone who had hidden from life behind the safety of a book and lived a great distance from her parents because she couldn't measure up to their expectations or stand up to their overbearing authority.

That person was no longer she. Diedre Forsythe was strong. She was a survivor. She lived off the land

and shared her life with a man who evoked equal measures of respect and longing and laughter.

And fear.

Sterling did frighten her, and not just a little. Did he guess it? Did he know he made her frightened of herself? There was an edge between them that was emotional, sexual, and a little dark because it burned so deep. What awaited her there beckoned like an abyss rippling with pleasures that had no limit because nothing was forbidden. The temptation to step off the ledge and plummet blindly into a savage Eden had been very real when he'd confronted her several days ago.

She had been only partially honest with him.

Yes, the possible repercussions to their friendship, which she prized dearly and would do anything to protect, made her wary. And yes, the memory of their frantic grappling against the tree, their white-hot encounter that had seared through the leash of civilized behavior and set loose primal urges, held her back. But what she hadn't told him was that the memory still had the power to weaken her knees, tighten her belly, and make her feel her own quickening moisture.

The way he looked at her when they said good night always commanded the same reaction. There was a ravenous hunger barely contained in his wise, fathomless eyes. She could almost see him visualizing his possession of her body and willing her to see it too. What she saw was as frightful as it was arousing.

Her virgin skin pierced under the onslaught of his masterful, unchecked seduction. An untamed ravishment of her body, her senses, and ultimately her soul. Any less would not appease him, and they both knew it.

Arousal. Fear. She didn't know anymore where one began and the other ended. They entwined and sparked a need so gripping, it was too overwhelming to confront.

Maybe she hadn't changed completely. She was still hiding from the inevitable, from a promise of fate that edged closer with each passing day.

Diedre shuddered. It was all too much.

And not enough.

She tickled her nose with her rabbit's foot, then kissed it.

"You're my good-luck charm," she confided. "First we'll take a swim, and then we'll go fishing. I feel a prize catch coming our way."

She giggled as she jumped to her feet and stretched. Oh, the power. She could feel the increasing physical strength in her taut muscles, and experienced a heady rush, as though sake were running through her veins. Not that she'd ever tasted the stuff. But Sterling had assured her it was pretty damn potent. He'd also promised her they'd share a whole bottle if they were ever rescued—or if he could find some wild rice to ferment himself on their island.

Since he was always close by, Diedre glanced around to make sure he was nowhere in sight before she stripped off what was left of her shirt. She would wash it along with her bra tomorrow with the camper's soap Sterling said he was busy brewing. Brewing. That meant a pot over a fire, didn't it? She would give her right arm for the luxury of having a pot.

She undid her clean but ragged white pants and peeled them off. Diedre caught her breath. The crotch was stained with red.

Her period. She clamped a hand over her mouth so she couldn't shriek and bring him running.

"Oh Lord," she whispered softly. "What am I going to do?" She pulled up her pants with a jerk and sank to the ground.

Holding her head in her hands, she could only wonder why she hadn't thought of this before. There was no store to meet her needs. Sterling would see her condition. The realization put her in a state of extreme distress. No, she wasn't distressed, she was mortified.

Hadn't her family shunned such indelicate matters? The word *period* was never even uttered in front of her father. When her monthly cycles first started, her mother had simply handed her a box and looked away in embarrassment. They'd never even discussed the birds and bees. Like everything else defining their relationship, that had been handled with utmost discretion. A book simply appeared one day on her bed, the one with fresh sheets tucked in daily by their maid.

She wanted to cry. She wanted to hide. Deciding if she stayed put, Sterling would find her, she quickly scrambled to her feet and began to look around. For what she didn't know. Just some clue to solve her horrible dilemma.

She found nothing. Her fear of exposure climbed to a point nearing anguish. Maybe she could find a hiding place where she could burrow in until she came to grips with her shame or hit on a solution. She began to look earnestly for signs of shelter, using the lessons Sterling had taught her so well.

Diedre spotted an outcropping of rocks covered by flowering vines and withered leaves. She began to push them away, clawing at them with her hands like a hunted prey seeking safety. When she managed to clear a small opening, she started to breathe easier. Hidden beneath the crawling vines was a small cave with enough room to easily accommodate one person.

Once more, she worked at the foliage, careful to leave as much of the camouflage as she could. She quickly scanned for snakes or rats inside. None, thank God. There were some bugs and spiders, but she got rid of those by wrapping her shirt around her wrist and pounding the insects.

Gasping from the exertion, she swept them out with her stained blouse, then crawled inside, drawing the natural curtain closed. She leaned against the solid wall of jagged rocks. After her eyes adjusted to the near-total darkness, she looked around and saw nothing spectacular. She stretched her limbs. Her feet reached to the opposite wall. The left middle finger touched stone on the farthest end of the cave. The other felt vines.

The shelter wasn't much, but it was something. A haven. Her place. Not a bad island pad.

She wouldn't tell Sterling, she decided. They shared everything else, but this would be just hers.

"Diedre!"

She curled up, pulling herself in as much as possible.

"Diedre! Dammit, answer me!"

He stopped near her hideaway. She couldn't exactly see him, but they were becoming so attuned to each other, she could feel his presence.

Would he feel hers? She bit her fist and prayed he'd go on. Diedre thought she heard him utter a mighty bad word before he moved on and his voice faded, though he called to her with more urgency.

She didn't have much time. He was sure to come back once he picked up her trail, and when he did, he was going to be madder than hell if he found out she was hiding from him.

Unfortunately, she couldn't camp here for the next week until the problem solved itself. There weren't many options available to her. She had no choice but to explain—as if he wouldn't see the proof for himself. Her only hope was that with all his skills, he might have a solution.

She cringed. Her modesty was at stake. None of the

trials she'd endured approached the magnitude of this, not even killing the rabbit.

Bracing herself for the most excruciating confrontation of her life, Diedre forced her feet away from the wall and crawled to the opening. Peeking through, she saw all was clear. She carefully pushed the curtain aside, then emerged on shaking limbs. Hearing his voice draw near again, she quickly concealed the opening, then darted toward the lagoon.

By the time she reached it, she was winded.

"Diedre!"

Drawing a deep breath, she called back, "Here! The lagoon!" Unable to bear the thought of his seeing her stained pants, she dived into the crystal-clear water.

"Where were you?" he demanded, striding angrily over pebbles and sand. "I was worried about—"

He went stone-still. She glanced around to see if danger lurked near.

It did. *He* was the danger. He was staring hard at her, his eyes taking on a torched and tortured cast. His jaw tensed, and his body stiffened. Even from the short distance she could see him begin to breathe in a short, ragged way that was close to a pant.

"You look good without your shirt," he said, his voice rough, strained. "But I'd stake my life that you look even better without that bra."

Diedre covered herself with her hands. Oh Lord, she'd left her shirt behind, covered with bugs and spiders! She hadn't remembered, she hadn't thought—

She took a halting step back. Her knees nearly buckled, then locked when she almost went under.

"Seeing you touch yourself like that . . . God, my hands should be there, not yours."

Her toes dug into the sandy bottom. Any fear she'd felt being with him receded to nothing as she came face to face with stark, heart-pounding terror.

"Quit hiding yourself from me," he said hoarsely. "Move your hands. Let me see."

She shook her head, her throat closing too tight to speak.

"Move them," he said. He took a step closer, his feet touching the lagoon's shallow end. "Please, Diedre. The hands. *Now*."

Her fingers were stiff as they gripped her breasts. He took another step, and she jerked her hands away, fearful he would do it for her if she didn't obey.

"The bra. Take off the bra."

"Sterling . . . no."

"Yes. Do this for me."

His eyes were alight with hunger, with longing. And something more that she was too shaken to define. She was scared. Dear God, she was scared out of her wits. She was also beginning to feel an unfurling excitement that reached up from the deepness of womanly need. Feeling her thighs begin to quiver, she braced to touch the realm of compelling unknowns. It was dizzying darkness. And blinding light.

She reached back with numb fingers. Shutting her eyes, she unfastened the bra. The water buoyed her unbound breasts; she could feel them floating, seemingly weightless. Embracing the light, she shed the cotton garment, felt it drift from her fingers and take something of her old self away.

Holding her gaze, Sterling moved forward. He drew nearer, nearer, keeping her still with some elusive power.

His toes touched hers. His hands embraced her face, then slid lightly over her throat . . . down to her breasts. His gaze followed the path, and her heart beat too fast. The water was cool, but his touch was hot.

"You feel like silk." His palms cupped her. "You fit in my hands just right. Like I knew you would. Round, full . . . ripe." He stroked a thumb over her taut, beaded nipple and whispered, "An uncultured pearl. One that's priceless, and waiting for me to claim it."

He bent his head, and she felt ricocheting sensations as his mouth covered her breast and tongue greeted nipple.

She made a whimpering sound that might have been his name. Her hands moved of their own volition, clasping his head to pull him closer, so she could sink deeper into his riveting hold. He worked his mouth around her, mastering her needs. Then to make up for his neglect of the other, he played it differently, toying, teasing, and then consuming with a rapacious greed.

She stretched her arms up, reaching for the sky, absorbing the streaking sensations and giving him full right.

He was thorough. He was insatiable. And so was she.

She felt him leave her and urgently tried to put him back. He obliged with a wet, lingering kiss, then slid up until they were chest to chest. His hands found hers, and they shared a oneness of need. Then he bent down, fitting his groin into the cradle of her thighs.

"Diedre," he murmured. "You're driving me crazy. I can't sleep. I can't think. All I can do is imagine filling you up with me. It's right, darlin', and I don't know how much longer I can wait."

Even through their clothes she felt him pulse and lift against her. She pulsed too. Her womb reached . . . and grasped nothing.

And then she remembered.

"I . . . " She swallowed hard and tried to forget her frantic need to hide. Why had she hidden from him? Sterling would never subject her to anything but his special gift for seeing in a way that others did not.

But at the moment he seemed to be seeing nothing

but her breasts, the urgent call to mate. His hands moved and fanned possessively over her buttocks. He kneaded her pliable flesh while his thighs gripped hers, holding her captive as he began to rub and thrust.

"Can you feel how hard you make me?"

"Yes," she whispered, clinging to his tense shoulders.

He slid his fingers below the band of her pants and grasped the metal zipper.

She was trapped between want and distress. She tried to twist away, but he stayed her with an iron-tight grip.

"No, Sterling," she cried urgently. "No! You can't."

"Easy," he whispered, gentling her frantic attempts to escape. "I know you're a virgin. I'll make it good for you. We'll fit together like a hand in a glove."

She had no choice. The words broke from her lips, stumbling out before it was too late to stop them.

"My period. It started today."

He stopped pulling down her zipper. He shut his eyes, and for a moment she grappled with the terrible possibility that he was repulsed.

But then he opened them again, and she saw not only his need to possess but . . . kindness. Sympathetic understanding.

"Were you hiding from me? Is that why I couldn't find you?"

She nodded her head. "I didn't want you to see."

"You were upset."

"I didn't know what to do. I still don't."

"You should have told me." He pulled up her zipper and gently cupped her face. "Diedre, don't you know by now that you can tell me anything?"

She realized then that it was true. She *could* tell him anything, even this, and he would offer only help and acceptance.

"What do I do, Sterling? There's no store around, or even a bathroom—"

"Shhh." He pressed two fingers against her mouth, then kissed her sweetly. "It's nature's way, and as old as time. Women didn't always have modern conveniences, so they made do with less. Indian women had a trick, and I don't think they'd mind my sharing it with you. You stay here, and I'll be right back."

He started to turn away, but Diedre caught his arm and stopped him. A flush stole into her cheeks, and she glanced down.

"Thank you, Sterling. You're a very special man."

"Takes a special woman to hook a special man." He tilted her chin up until she looked at him. "Put aside your embarrassment. What distinguishes a woman from a man is a beautiful thing, really. Even intriguing. Like you."

He was the intriguing one, she thought. Even now this marvelous man made her smile, made her wonder why she had been so distressed. It was because of her old life, of course, and the set of values that had been ingrained into her that now seemed wrong, a slur on nature's integrity.

"I wasn't raised to accept all of myself."

"It's a shame. I'll bet you didn't know that in some primitive cultures a girl's first menses is regarded as a great event. Hell, they even had a celebration." He tweaked her nose and grinned. "So . . . what d'ya say? Let's throw a party."

"A party!" she exclaimed, then laughed. "What kind of party?"

"Oh, just you and me. We won't invite any guests. I think it would be romantic dancing on the beach. You can sing to the moon. I won't kill the mood by joining in."

"Sterling, you're nuts! No wonder I—" *Love you.*

She swayed forward, listening to the whisper of her heart. Sterling's eyes narrowed, and he studied her with an eaglelike gaze. He seemed to see past all fronts right through to her soul.

Neither of them said anything in the silence. Then he touched her face and backed away. She let her gaze rove over the sleekness of hard muscle, the clinging grip of jeans to thighs.

Once on the bank, he turned. As quickly as he might throw a punch or strike with a lethal kick, the gentleness in his eyes reverted to a gleam of masculine prowess. His gaze raked over her naked breasts. His face was etched by the rawness of unsated need. He stared at her for a long time that way, until she sank down so the water lapped at her chin. When he finally spoke, his tone was serious.

"I have no aversion to lovemaking, whatever the time of the month. For that reason I'd advise you to get dressed while I'm gone. The tether's getting dangerously short, Diedre. I'm afraid it doesn't need much provocation to snap."

Diedre lay down on her pallet, watching Sterling. He was a study of symmetrical perfection as he stoked the fire, then took his rest on the other bed.

"I had a wonderful time tonight," she said quietly. "You're quite an accomplished dancer."

"You're not bad yourself, darlin'. You move with me like a shadow, and you sing like an angel."

She exulted in his praise, and her heart flew on a wing. Oh, how they'd danced as she'd sung to the moon and stars. No black-tie dinner could ever rival the splendor of their party for two.

She told him that with her gaze, letting him see the love she hadn't spoken but couldn't hide. Did he love her too? Perhaps there was more than a chance that he did. How many men would go to the trouble to gather pennyroyal and red raspberry leaf to ease a woman's cramp?

Diedre shifted and smiled. The G-string fit snugly against her hips, and the thong filled with dry grass took her flow.

She reached across the short distance that kept them apart. Sterling met her halfway and closed the space that she knew would soon be removed.

His hand covered hers, their fingers interlocked. They fell asleep cocooned by nature's sanctuary and joined by their silent, unbreakable bond.

Nine

Diedre wrung out her shirt as she knelt by the lagoon. Holding it up for inspection, she shook her head. There was no help for it. The garment couldn't be cleaner, thanks to Sterling's gift of camper's soap, which she'd been using for the past two weeks to bathe and do the wash with. He'd said it was made by boiling fat, water, and wood ashes. What he had boiled it in, she had no idea. But she knew her shirt had had it. It had more holes than material.

Her pants weren't in much better shape, and she found damn little comfort in that. The dark edge of desire between her and Sterling was growing to dangerous proportions, and starting to eclipse their friendship. Lately, he was short-tempered; she was inclined to snap back. His heavy, taut silences and the naked, carnal stares she endured for heart-palpitating minutes at a time did nothing to diminish her panic. The warning was unspoken but crystal-ball clear: His shortening tether could snap at any time.

She was certain that prancing around in her bra and panties would slice the straining rope. Her clothes, or what was left of them, provided little cover, but they were all she had.

A dark, rolling cloud smothered the high noon sun. Diedre looked up at the same time she heard the sudden rumble of thunder. She got up. Sterling had warned her about storms in the Devil's Triangle, the ones that came without warning, shrieking and destroying before departing as quickly as they commenced.

Storms like the one that had driven them here.

The threat was enough to make her forget about her clothing dilemma. Wasting no time, she was already scaling the towering rocks on the bluff when the first blast hit. There was no prelude of light rain, only a gush from the belching sky. Her fingers slid on the wet stones, and she tumbled down, scraping her bare waist against the jagged edges.

"Sterling!" she screamed but the name was thrown back into her face by an angry gust of wind. She was already drenched to the bone as she scrambled to regain her footing. Her hair streamed over her eyes, and she thought she was crying. Her chest heaved on a sob while pelting rain stung her cheeks.

She had to get away from the lagoon, which was no longer a haven but a dangerous pool. It was imperative to find shelter before she was beaten down. Her place was much closer than their camp.

Diedre changed course, charging against the raging onslaught. A vicious growl of thunder resounded just before a streak of jagged lightning arced a pointed path and struck not twenty feet away.

Her hair bristled, and her ears rang with the deafening crack. Dazed, she felt the ground being ripped by the electrical current.

She began to crawl, feeling like the rabbit hunted and destined for slaughter by a force more powerful than she. She focused on her hiding place. It wasn't far, though it seemed miles away.

She reached the edge of the jungle. The swirling branches were like vegetation being pulped in a massive blender, threatening to suffocate her. Suddenly, a hard weight came down on her shoulder. She shrieked, expecting to feel the impact of a fallen tree.

But, suddenly, she was being lifted, and Sterling was grasping her against him. She looked up into his rain-battered face.

"You're safe," he said. She couldn't hear him over the howling torrent, but she could read his lips. And she could feel harbor in his powerful, protective arms. She clung to him, burying her face against his wet neck. He forged ahead purposefully, fighting the enemy with his own formidable strength.

The sounds of nature's unrestrained malice echoed in her ears. She could smell and taste the downpour mingling with Sterling's sweat. She could feel branches slapping against her while he tried to shelter her back with his hands.

It seemed an eternity before she realized they were insulated from the elements. Diedre pried her face from his shoulder. His skin bore minor scratches, as if he'd tangled with a cat. She could hear him breathing harshly while the wailing wind cried mournfully outside.

"Where are we?" Her voice shook as much as she.

He smiled. "Welcome home. I planned to carry you over the threshold, but this wasn't exactly what I had in mind."

He set her down, and she sank onto a hard, smooth floor. Sterling joined her, dropping to his knees, his chin falling to his chest. She could see his muscles quivering while he breathed in deep, ragged breaths.

Diedre took her gaze off her protector long enough to look past him to a wide opening. The storm raged brutally, but the mouth of rocks refused to give it entry.

"A cave!"

"Shut your eyes," he said firmly, stroking thumb and forefinger over her lids. "I need a little rest before I give you a tour."

"A tour?" She could almost forget their lashing as excitement took hold. "You mean—"

"You'll see. It's a surprise."

Diedre tried her best to obey as she felt him stretch and heard his breathing return to normal. But curiosity won out, and she squinted through the cover of her lashes.

"Uh-uh. It's not fair if you peek."

She quickly shut her eyes tight. Even when Sterling was teasing, his authority brooked no contention.

She felt him slide an arm beneath her legs, lift her to his chest, and carry her. Wherever he was taking her to smelled a little damp, musty. It also seemed tight, close, still.

"Now," he said. "Open your eyes."

Diedre blinked several times, adjusting from darkness to muted light. They were a little nearer to the opening, she realized. There was a recess in the rock wall, and framing it were wooden stakes sunk into transplanted soil and lashed to a crossbar of saplings. On the floor beneath was gravel spread over what looked like a layer of dirt.

"A fireplace. Should be pretty cozy on a rainy day like this."

"A fireplace!" she exclaimed.

"Well, not exactly the type you'd find in Hyannis Port. But it's a far cry better than the one we've got on shore."

"Oh, Sterling," she cried. "It's wonderful, it's fabulous, it's—"

"Now, don't get carried away. There's a few more things to see, and you don't want to exhaust your vocabulary before I'm through."

He slid her down his length, and she made no

attempt to disguise how thrilled she was—or that she absolutely, positively adored him.

"What else?" she asked, trying hard not to jump up and down in her excitement.

"How about . . . " Swiftly he bent down and presented her with a large, funny-looking wooden container. "A kettle. It's treated so it won't burn when we put it on the fireplace."

"A pot! You made me a pot!" She stood on tiptoe and rained kisses on his face. "Oh, you gorgeous man! You wonderful, sweet—"

"Savage," he reminded her before capturing her mouth with a hard, possessive kiss. She was returning it with equal fervor and was ready to climb all over him when he broke it off.

"Diedre," he warned, a hungry glint simmering in his eyes, "I'm *not* sweet. I'm a man who's on the verge of ravishing your body with such force that that storm's only a whimper in comparison. Unless you're in the mood to be a virgin sacrifice, you'd better tone down the next kiss, or we won't finish the tour."

"Sorry," she said, not feeling contrite.

Sterling shook his head as if to clear it, then led her by the hand to the middle of the cave.

"Next stop, the boudoir," he said in a low, rough voice. Gesturing to two pallets that lay close together but not quite side by side, he eyed her intently. "Single beds, but we'll put them together *soon* and make a double."

Even in her euphoric state, she couldn't mistake the thread of certainty and gnawing impatience in him. She felt the familiar, taut twining of apprehension and anticipation snake through her belly and twist in the pit of her stomach.

Sterling all but yanked her behind him as he strode to the end of the large cave. "Now, what have we here?" he asked, pointing to a handmade vat.

"I don't know. You tell me."

"What? Can't you tell? The wine cellar, of course, *madame*."

"*Mademoiselle*," she corrected automatically, her sureness coming from four years of French lessons. "The difference is that one's married and the other one's—"

"I know the difference." His eyes narrowed and he said firmly, "*Madame*."

He was staring at her so intently that she began to feel uncomfortable. She broke the visual contact and shifted her attention to the vat. "Do you have wine in there?"

"Close," he said, drumming his fingers on the cover. "Berries and other assorted ingredients in a questionable chemical state. It needs more time to ferment, but I'm tempted to give it a try tonight." His gaze slid over her, then backtracked to linger on her bra-covered chest. "Maybe it'll take the edge off, and I can sleep for a change."

Diedre crossed her arms in reflex. Her first thought was that the edge might cave in with a push from his homemade booze. Her imagination took flight, envisioning Sterling freed from his self-imposed control and aggressively claiming his primal rights.

She shivered.

"You're cold," he said, running his palms briskly over her arms. The brisk movements lessened to a stroke, and the stroke became a caress.

"I saved the best for last," he murmured. With a seductive smile he leaned down and presented her with two pieces of tanned pelts. "*Voilà*. New clothes."

He placed them into her hands. Tears immediately welled in and fell from her astonished eyes.

"I can't believe it. You even made me clothes?"

"They're sturdy, even if they aren't too fashionable. But I'm sure on you they'll look—" He seemed to mentally strip her before he let out a low, masculine chuckle. "Let's just say I think you could only look better in nothing."

She hugged the garments to her, stroking them as her heart swelled. She'd been given many extravagant gifts throughout her privileged life, but next to this they paled, like flimsy trinkets compared to diamonds.

"They're beautiful, Sterling. I can never thank you enough."

"Sure you can. Try them on while I go make a fire." As he pivoted, he said quietly, "Don't worry. I won't look."

Diedre watched his retreating back. She wanted to rush to him. She wanted to kiss him.

She wanted to try on her new clothes.

Once she was certain Sterling was concentrating on his task, she went to the farthest end of the cave for privacy. With only the faintest light, she saw that he'd fashioned her a bodice and a matching pair of shorts.

They were short all right, with snakeskin lacing down the sides to hold them together. She inspected the crotch and was a little taken aback to realize it was wide and full. While it would allow free movement to chase prey, it wasn't very conducive to sitting cross-legged, or scaling a tree if he was on the ground looking up.

Diedre's mouth gaped open. Wide-eyed, she looked from the outfit to Sterling. *Good Lord!* Had he taken design lessons from Fredrick's of Hollywood?

But he had made them just for her. She felt a pang of guilt for her momentary lack of gratefulness.

Deciding the bodice would cover a little bit more—a very little bit more—she shrugged off the wet bra, then shimmied into her new top.

She ran her hands over the soft, suedelike leather. Her breasts swung free, and her nipples brushed against the supple pelt. It felt . . . wonderful. Exotic. Almost sinful and strangely . . . arousing.

Had he been aroused as he'd cut and pieced to a nearly perfect fit? Had he imagined her naked shape, or pretended he was the pelt destined to cloak her skin?

Diedre suddenly realized she was running her palms over her breasts and wishing the palms were his. She stared in disbelief at her hands. She jerked them away, shocked by her actions. They were primitive, sexual, and distinctly different from any way she'd touched herself before.

He could have seen! He stood only about ten long strides from her

Who was she? A flash of the cultured woman she'd been clashed with this woman who was fondling herself and fantasizing about the man nearby.

Shaken, Diedre hastily exchanged her tattered pants and soaked undies for the revealing but dry shorts. She didn't give herself the opportunity to explore the feel of suede between her thighs, and instead marched straight to Sterling.

He turned.

Oh, sweet Father, what was I thinking of when I put together something like that?

Sterling could feel his Adam's apple lodge in a suddenly parched throat.

"That's . . . uh . . . " He swallowed hard. "I see it fits. Maybe . . . a little too well?"

"It's comfortable." She ran her palms over her hips, then abruptly stopped. "You did a good job."

Sterling nodded, unable to speak a word. Deciding he was close to losing control, he quickly jerked his attention back to the fire.

"Tell you what. We'll settle for some jerky I've got stored with some dried fruit. It's in a corner at the back. You go get it while I change."

"You made yourself something too?"

"Matching outfits, darlin'," he said between a groan and a sigh. "These pants have had it, and I'm tired of wearing the damn things. You don't mind, do you?"

He stole a sideways glance at her and immediately regretted it. She was stroking her fingertips over the shorts and looking at him with an almost dazed expression. Then she snatched her hands away.

"Of course I don't mind. Go ahead." She turned away and said in a throaty voice, "Don't worry. I won't look."

"You can if you want to."

She stopped. She hesitated. Then she shook her head and walked away.

His gaze followed the sway of her hips, the endless length from thigh to ankle. Sterling jerked his hungry gaze back to the fire, and then out to the retreating storm.

What he felt rushing through his veins was enough to make his earlier battle against nature seem tame. His need had grown from a ceaseless gnawing to a ravenous desire.

He was no ninja with a pureness of spirit to command his mind and body. He was no warrior committed to the path. He was a man driven to quench an out-of-control fire.

He didn't trust himself. For Diedre's sake, that scared him, because he loved her, perhaps too much.

With a growl and curse he quickly stripped, then donned his new clothes. His shorts, which were more like a loincloth, could not conceal his arousal. And there was nothing he could do to disguise it.

He strode past Diedre, unwilling to chance a fleeting glance at her, and headed straight for the wine. He hoped it was strong. With any luck he'd pass out before he attacked her.

Diedre caught his arm, and he exhaled an expletive.

"I found the jerky and fruit. Where do you want to eat?"

"Outside. By the fire. Anywhere. Just don't make it on the bed."

He speared her eyes with laser-sharp message. She let go of his arm and stepped back.

"Meet you by the fire," she said in a soft voice. Too soft. As soft as her womanflesh that he was close to manhandling in no gentle way.

Sterling went straight for the liquid sustenance. Lifting the rough wood cover, he ducked his head and sipped. Tart. Bitter. The first alcohol he'd consumed in nearly two months, it went straight to his head and made his toes tingle. It also managed to give him back some control over his body.

He drank freely and certainly not gracefully. More like a dog to his bowl than a connoisseur to crystal.

Feeling as though he'd downed a case in ten gulps, and vastly relieved to get even a tenuous hold of himself, he called to his woman. That's right—*his* woman.

"Hey, Diedre. Come get a mouthful of this."

Even in his semi-inebriated state, he picked up the sound of footsteps over smooth, flat rock.

"Don't you want to eat something?" she asked.

"Nah. I'd rather drink. C'mon, join me."

She stooped down but came to a halt before her lips touched the beverage.

"I don't suppose you have a glass?"

Sterling threw back his head and laughed. Boy, did he get a kick out of her.

"I've got a few coconut shells. I'll give you one on a condition."

She stared at him warily.

"Not that. I just want to see you shed the last of civilization and guzzle straight from the barrel."

Diedre seemed to consider his offer.

"If I guzzle, you'll give me a cup?"

"Darlin', you've got my word. A man's only as good as that."

She looked from him to the open container. Then she smiled and said, "Hey, why not?"

Sterling watched the dip of her head, then quickly gathered her hair before it fell in. He heard her delicate sips, followed by a choke and a cough.

"Good night! What the hell's in there?"

"I already told ya. Bet it damn near knocked your socks off."

Diedre giggled and straightened. "Okay, I guzzled. Now, where's my cup?"

"Two cups, comin' right up." Sterling fetched them and served the lady first. She seemed to brace herself before taking a swig. "How's the bouquet?" he asked.

Diedre swirled the berry wine and sniffed it.

"Well . . . it's strong. But interesting."

"A tad rough?"

"I guess you could say that. Reminds me a little of you. Not exactly kosher, but definitely intoxicating."

Her eyes met his over the brown hull. She either blinked several times or batted her lashes.

It occurred to him that Diedre probably had less tolerance than he did. He wasn't too proud of it, but he'd gotten more than one girl drunk in his lifetime to gain the advantage.

Diedre wasn't just any girl. And he'd never been possessed by a woman the way he was possessed by her.

"Drink up, darlin'," he urged, tilting the hull to her lush, wine-wet mouth. "There's plenty more where that came from."

Ten

Sterling watched the liquid meet her mouth. He quickly filled his own shell and tapped it to hers.

"Shall I propose a toast?" he asked.

"No. *I'll* propose the toast." She touched his lips with her fingers. "Here's to our lovely new home. *And* to the man who made it."

"And to the woman who gave him the reason to make it."

They hooked arms, then gazed at each other as they sipped their wine. Feeling himself get lost in those big baby blues, Sterling decided that getting Diedre loose was quickly becoming more of a mandate than an idea.

"What do you like best?" He leaned down to lap a stray drop trickling down her chin.

"Mmm . . . that's easy." She kissed the tip of his tongue, then murmured, "What I like best is you."

That did it. Come hell or high water, he was bedding her tonight. But taking advantage of her relaxed senses wasn't good enough. The least she deserved was a seduction.

"I bet you'll like me even better after I give you the most special present of all."

"More? Sterling, you've given me so much as it is, what more could I want?"

Guilt. It hit him without mercy or regard for the discipline he'd exercised over his raging passion for an innocent woman. Maybe a seduction wasn't good enough either.

Setting aside their cups, he led her to the fire. From a nearby rock shelf he picked up his final gift. He urged her to sit close to the heat and realized the storm had receded. A balmy night was descending and the fragrance of a fresh breeze seemed to sigh its relief.

He faced her, knee touching knee, gaze meeting gaze.

"For you." He extended his lover's entreaty, wrought by his hands and coming straight from the heart.

"A comb!" She stared at the hardened, polished spine of a large fish as if it were a treasure chest filled with rubies and jewels.

"Two." He pressed into her hand a carved abalone shell. "The comb gets the tangles out, while this keeps hair out of the way. Functional and decorative too."

"They're . . . beautiful, the most beautiful things I've ever seen. They're perfect." She glanced down at her outfit, and then he thought her eyes strayed to his own short garment. "Well, almost."

"Nothing but the best for you, darlin'."

His raging lust, his endless need, melted in the bottomless reaches of his heart.

"What say we give it a try?" he asked.

Diedre needed no more prompting and sank the comb into her hair. She pulled. She tugged. She yanked.

"Stuck. It's been too long since I had a brush."

"Here. Sit in front of me, and I'll do it."

"You don't mind?"

"Hardly," he said, laughing. "I've been wanting to

get my hands in your hair forever." He scooted until his groin rested against her tailbone and his thighs cupped her hips. She nuzzled in closer.

He went from hard to stone-hard. Seduction became tantamount.

He stroked the long, wild mane between his fingers, then massaged her temples until she leaned back and exhaled a soft, delighted sigh. Taking the comb, he began to work from the ends up.

"How did you become a ninja?" she said, the words a bit slurred.

He hit a tangle as well as an old, insurmountable obstacle.

"I'm not there yet." His jaw clenched tight while he fingered the bleached strands. "I don't know if I'll ever be."

"But you know the techniques. You even taught me how to throw someone twice my size."

"It's more than that, Diedre. To be a true ninja, you must be strong. Believe me, I'm not always strong. Sometimes I'm terribly weak. *You* make me weak."

"Do I? I'm glad. Mmm . . . that feels wonderful, Sterling." She relaxed against him with a purr. "You never told me how you met the Grandmaster. He didn't teach you how to brush a woman's hair, did he? If he did, he taught you *very, very* well."

"No, he didn't teach me this. But he taught me most everything else."

"But how did you meet him? Was it by chance or—ouch!"

"Sorry." He drew back her hair to kiss her neck in apology for his roughness. It wasn't Diedre's fault the subject was a delicate one for him. How much should he confess? He supposed he could tell her parts of the story and allay her curiosity without breaking the cozy mood or introducing a stumbling block to their relationship.

"It was over ten years ago," he said, drifting back to another lifetime, another world.

"You must have been in the service then."

"That's right. I came in after Nam, so I wasn't in the thick of action. Mostly, I was training friendlies, certain U.S. allies, in guerrilla-warfare tactics." He wouldn't mention he'd been trained to be a human killing machine and that he'd been spawning more like himself. Sterling's face hardened.

"At the time we'd just completed a mission to . . . let's say, deal with some terrorists. We were successful, and I was feeling my oats, so I went to Japan on R and R. Thought I'd take in the sights, drink some sake—" *Bed a few women to get the men whose throats I'd slit out of my system.*

"And you met him there?"

"Not right away." He hit an ungiving tangle and reached for his knife. Slicing the knotted hair, he put it aside with the blade and worked the comb up an inch. "I'd been there about a week, and my time was nearly up, when I came out of a bar and saw a bunch of GIs roughing up a local girl. Made me see red."

Diedre gasped with shock.

"I suspected they had something a lot more brutal in mind. Fighting and killing can mess with people's sense of right and wrong. Maybe that's when I decided I was getting out as soon as my enlistment was up."

"You never talk about the time you served."

"Not much to talk about. The Berets weren't exactly going great guns then, so I got out during the lull. There's never been any love lost between the Special Forces and regular military. Anything, anytime, anyplace, anyhow, was our motto, and a lot of people pretty much looked at us as a bunch of bastard renegades."

Diedre went very still while he sliced off another matted curl.

"All things considered, I didn't feel bad when I hung up my beret. I wasn't needed that much."

"I need you." She yawned. "So what happened that night, anyway?"

"I interceded. There were four against me, and I decked two of them. Before I could take the others on, a short, older man came on the scene." The memory was as fresh as though it had happened only yesterday.

"Was it the Grandmaster?" She yawned again and leaned closer to his chest.

"I didn't know him as such then, but I do remember his power, and the awe I felt watching him move faster than light. I'd been trained by the best, and here I was eating his dust. Before I could blink, those SOBs were scattered all over the ground. I think my jaw must have dropped to my feet. Then he bowed to me. Quick but graceful. Courtly. When he straightened, he looked at me in a way I'll never forget."

"Was it strange?" she murmured faintly.

"I'll say. He looked at me like he'd known me all his life. And then he clamped his hand on my shoulder and said, '*Onushi dekiruna.*' I found out later that meant he felt that he knew me." Sterling nuzzled his nose against her hair. It smelled of rain and herbal fragrance. He whispered against the heady silkiness, "It was the way I felt when I first touched you."

"Ahh . . ." She sighed. "And the girl . . . ? Was she all right?"

"She was pretty shaken up, but fine. She turned out to be his granddaughter. Ming was her name." He tensed and pulled Diedre closer. He hadn't said his fiancée's name in what seemed like ages. She had no place between him and Diedre, no part in the specialness they shared.

"And so you saved Ming. What happened to her?"

"She grew up." *With a fixation on me.* He remembered how she'd waited on him hand and foot, her tilted doe eyes gazing at him as if he were the hero he knew he really wasn't. She'd looked at him that way for the rest of his leave, and then later, when he'd returned to study under her grandfather.

Deciding he wanted to put the story to an immediate end, he concluded, "Anyway, the Grandmaster asked me to share a cup of sake, and the rest is what you might call history."

He pulled a final stroke through the glorious waves of her untangled hair, and Diedre's head fell back against his shoulder.

"Gorgeous," he whispered, pressing his lips against her temple while he put aside the comb. He noticed she still grasped the abalone shell in a loose fist.

"Enough about me and my past." He slid his hand up the arched length of her neck. "All I care about is you and us, the here and now. About what we feel for each other and the way I want to spend the rest of our lives together."

He grazed his fingertips up her rib cage, frowning when he encountered a small welt. He would tend to it later. He moved upward and encountered no resistance from Diedre. The wine had worked its magic, it seemed, aiding his imminent seduction.

Her breast filled his palm with a swelling heat. Rubbing his thumb back and forth over her nipple, he was rewarded with their hardening thrust.

"It's time, darlin'," he murmured. "Let's go to bed."

Her only response was a sleep-laden sigh followed by a soft, tiny snore. Sterling stared down in disbelief at her peaceful, trusting face.

She'd passed out. His ploy to get her loose so he could have his way had backfired. Damn! He couldn't believe it! He was stiffer than starch, her behind softer than feathered down, and she was as unconscious as the day he'd touched her in the glade.

He could do it now. But that wouldn't be good enough. Not even half good enough. He wanted her responsive, willing. He wanted to hear her scream, feel her shake and take him until he touched her womb.

Sterling groaned and dropped his chin to her head. Every blue word he'd ever learned in the military surged through his head. In his condition he wouldn't be able to sleep, as if he'd had a decent night's sleep since they'd been stranded.

His frustration hit a new high. At this point his wisest course of action would be to guzzle enough wine to put him out of his misery. He was almost choking on the urge to forget how he wanted her and to settle for what his male needs dictated he *must* have and must take any way he could.

With Herculean effort Sterling set his desire aside. He pried the abalone comb from Diedre's fingers and nestled it into her hair. He got up with a long-suffering sigh, then carried Diedre to her pallet and gently put her down.

His next stop was the watering hole. He imbibed several long gulps before putting back the lid.

The stuff was rotgut. If he didn't have a hangover tomorrow, it'd be a miracle. He stared long and hard at Diedre, fighting carnal thoughts. Once the wine hit him, he grabbed some salve and wove his way over to her bed.

He snarled at the sight of the separate pallets, then shoved them together. Dropping to his knees, he rolled her over and pushed the bodice all the way up. A quick glance assured him the welt was very small. While he stroked the balm over it his eyes feasted on her breasts.

He finished with his ministrations, then lay down beside her. He dreamed of fondling her freely, of molding the ivory orbs however he wanted. He wanted too much. He imagined his mouth coming down until it was filled with her delicate flesh, and his tongue darting over her nipple, voracious and starved and frantic.

He fell asleep with a last coherent thought.

Today he'd brought his bride home and given her his offering of love. Tomorrow he would consummate his claim.

Diedre wasn't sure what woke her. Was it the midmorning light seeping into their cave? Or the slight throb in her temples?

She started to get up, but found herself pinned down by a weight. She lowered her gaze and saw Sterling's head cushioned on her chest and his parted mouth resting against a nipple.

Her eyes widened. Her top! It was pushed up to her neck. Sterling's doing while she was asleep, obviously. He shifted, and she realized one large leg was thrown over hers. Intimately, possessively. His upper thigh, sandwiched between her legs, had nudged aside her shorts and was pressed firmly against her feminine heat. His own aroused heat was barely covered by his shorts and was prodding her hip.

What had happened last night? She'd been a little woozy, but certainly conscious enough to know the difference between having her hair combed and rolling around in bed with him.

Apparently, he hadn't taken full advantage. They still had on their clothes, not that that could prevent them from performing the act, considering the brevity of their attire.

Sterling made a low groan in his sleep. He could wake any minute, she thought, and began to feel some alarm. If he woke up now, he'd have her under him before she could blink. He wouldn't ask. He would take. And the way he would take her would not be tame. She knew it with absolute certainty.

Her instinct for self-protection demanded that she

Passion awaits you...
Step into the magical world of

Loveswept

ENJOY...

6 ROMANCES RISK FREE!

PLUS

FREE GIFT

Enjoy Kay Hooper's *"Larger Than Life"*!
Not for sale anywhere, this exclusive
novel is yours to keep–FREE–
no matter what!

SEE DETAILS INSIDE...

A Magical World of Enchantment Awaits You When You're Loveswept!

Your heart will be swept away with Loveswept Romances when you meet exciting heroes you'll fall in love with...beautiful heroines you'll identify with. Share the laughter, tears and the passion of unforgettable couples as love works its magic spell. These romances will lift you into the exciting world of love, charm and enchantment!

You'll enjoy award-winning authors such as Iris Johansen, Sandra Brown, Kay Hooper and others who top the best-seller lists. Each offers a kaleidoscope of adventure and passion that will enthrall, excite and exhilarate you with the magic of being Loveswept!

- ♥ *We'd like to send you 6 new novels to enjoy–risk free!*
- ♥ *There's no obligation to buy.*
- ♥ *6 exciting romances–plus your free gift–brought right to your door!*
- ♥ *Convenient money-saving, time-saving home delivery!*

Join the Loveswept at-home reader service and we'll send you 6 new romances about once a month– before they appear in the bookstore! You always get 15 days to preview them before you decide. Keep only those you want. Each book is yours for only $2.25*. That's a total savings of $3.00 off the retail price for each 6 book shipment.

ENJOY . . .

♥ 6 Romance Novels–Risk Free! ♥ Exclusive Novel Free!
♥ Money Saving Home Delivery!

get free before it was too late. If she hid for a little while, he'd have a chance to collect himself and get a grip before he lost what little control she knew he had left.

Very carefully, she scooted her hips away from him. He made another low growl at the same time his leg clamped tighter over hers. Diedre didn't dare move. She waited for several seconds until his breathing settled into a steady, even tempo.

Her relief that he was still asleep was enormous. Gathering her courage, she tried again, this time moving her upper body first. She drew on the subtle techniques of movement he'd taught her, sliding as stealthily as the wind. Just as she got him off her breast, his head rolled sideways and almost landed on the floor.

She caught him, but just barely. Closing her eyes and taking a shallow breath, she gently laid his head on the cushion of leaves.

Her heart was hammering. Her legs were shaking, and she could only pray that his finely tuned senses wouldn't be alerted by the trembling. She rose, inch by inch, until she was sitting up. Bracing herself for the greatest challenge of all, she began to slide her hips away.

As she sought her freedom, her gaze fell on the protrusion in his shorts. She stared in awe and more than a little fear. He would put *that* in her? She stared in awe and more than a little fear.

Escape became no longer merely wise, but mandatory. Forcing herself to look away, she silently drew her body out from under him.

At last she was free! Then she saw him reach out, grasping the emptiness of her bed. Her heart raced, and seizing the chance, she sprang up and darted to the opening of the cave. She paused only long enough to steal a fleeting glance at him.

Sterling rolled over. He emitted a snore.

It was the sweetest sound she'd ever heard. On soundless feet she raced to safety.

Sterling felt for the body lying next to him. His hand touched a soft leaf but not soft skin. He began to search earnestly with his open palm, meaning to pull her back.

Nothing. His eyes snapped open, and he sat up with a jerk. Big mistake. The walls of Jericho caved in on his fuzzy brain, then went off like a bomb in his head.

"Diedre!" he called, pressing his hands to his throbbing temples. "Diedre, are you in here?"

Silence. She was gone.

He muttered a foul word, then got up. He didn't know what angered him more—that she'd got away or that his drinking binge had let her pull it off.

Flinging a slur at the keg, he set out to find her. He had a doozy of a hangover for sure, but he'd woken up just as needy as when he'd gone to bed. His drunken sleep had been riddled with erotic images. Hell, he was surprised he hadn't had a wet dream.

Outside, he picked up her track and followed it. He stopped near the lagoon and sniffed. The wind came from the east, and he caught the faintest whiff of human fragrance. The scent of woman.

His hangover receded with the mounting anticipation starting to flush through his veins. He was on her trail and closing fast.

Sterling paused behind a thicket of trees high over the narrow strip of pebbled sand. Branches littered the shore, testimony to the storm's abuse. He spotted her immediately. She was bent over, quickly sipping at the water as though she was in a hurry and had stopped just long enough to quench her thirst.

She cupped her palms and bathed her face. Suddenly she tilted her head back. His breathing quickened. Rivulets streamed over her face and trickled down her neck, only to disappear beneath the bodice. His fingers clenched, demanding that he remove that barrier to her nakedness.

Diedre went very still, and he could see her eyes darting around. Ah, yes, he had taught her well. The instinctiveness of her reaction only managed to cut through the frayed tether of his control.

They were like mirrors reflecting each other's thoughts, intents, and presence. *She* was his perfect mate. *He* was hers. Only one symbolic, physical act remained to seal the completeness of their bond.

His hand gravitated to the drawstring riding low on his hips while he moved steadily and soundlessly forward.

Diedre saw him the second he emerged from the cover of trees. She leaped to her feet and began to edge back, shaking her head *no* back and forth.

"Yes," he whispered to himself, locking his eyes on the juncture of her thighs before dropping from the rock ledge and landing easily on all fours.

In a flash she was running. Sterling picked up his pace. And he began to stalk her.

Eleven

The split second she saw him, she knew he was there for one purpose: to stake his claim. To mate.

Diedre could feel her heart pounding, and in spite of the water she'd just drunk, her throat was bone-dry. He was the hunter. She was the hunted. Sterling would seek, and he would find. She had no time to waste, or he would fell her to the ground.

Run! came the instinctive command. Her instincts had been honed well, and she didn't question them. Pebbles flew beneath her roughened feet, and she blessed the freedom the clothes provided.

Her mind clicked into survivor mode. The lagoon would provide no help—he could outswim her. Her only hope was to hide. He was stronger, faster. But she was smaller and could use that to her advantage.

Her place? She wouldn't be safe there for long. He would track her down, and she would no longer have a secret hideaway.

Darting for the jungle's interior, Diedre flew past trees so fast they were only a blur. Should she scale one and hope he'd lose her? *No.* Even if she could make her way to the top before he saw her, Sterling would sense her presence and she would be cornered.

The trees grew denser and she scanned for a familiar sight. Then she saw it—hallelujah!—an odd grouping of rocks that jutted skyward. There was a small tunnel between land and stone. Too small for him but not for her.

She plunged past draping ivy and exotic flowers, heedless of any toxic plant. Listening with the acute hearing of the hunted, she heard nothing. But that meant nothing. He could move silently, even blend so completely with nature as to render himself invisible. For that reason she didn't hesitate to burrow into the tunnel.

Diedre belatedly realized it was too shallow, no more than ten feet long. Her body took up a little over half of it, and she crawled by the strength of her fingers, not stopping until she was in far enough that he couldn't reach in and drag her out. She pressed her cheek to the ground and took quick gulps of air.

Suddenly, she heard a sound. An unmistakable hiss. She stopped breathing. Good God, what had she been thinking in her mad flight? There could be snakes in here!

What was the greater danger? A snake could kill her. Sterling would do what he wished with her body, but she wouldn't die.

At least, she didn't think she would. The memory of what had driven her out of the cave came to her. Her thighs protectively pressed tightly together. She began to crawl out, frantically hoping she wouldn't encounter a viper—be it serpent or man.

Reaching the tunnel's end with neither in sight, she gave a prayer of thanks along with a plea to let her escape. Diedre stuck out her head just far enough for her to look around. No sign of Sterling. Had she eluded him after all?

Stealthily, she pulled herself out and pressed her back against the rocks. She used every skill at her command, drawing on his ingrained teachings and working them against him. Not sensing him, she edged around the outcropping and checked every direction.

Just as she began to take off, something streaked down, dropping from the top of the tunnel and landing dead center in front of her.

"Going somewhere?" Sterling braced his hands on either side of her, imprisoning her against the stony wall.

She didn't have time to scream, to gasp, or to groan.

"Good thing there weren't any snakes in that tunnel. Otherwise, this little cat-and-mouse game would've been up sooner." He leaned closer to her. She could feel his heated breath graze her neck, making the fine hair stand on end. "Ssss," he hissed beside her ear.

Despite her terror she realized he'd been there all along and had flushed her out with the threat of a snake.

Diedre tried to duck beneath his arms and bolt. He caught her too easily, then pressed his palm between her breasts.

"Please," she begged. "Sterling, please, no. You frighten me."

His eyes were alight with carnal hunger. His fingers spread out, their span so large, he touched both her nipples. He began to rub them in a delicate, slow circular motion.

"Fear is your enemy, not me. Get rid of it, Diedre. The ritual's begun."

"Ritual?" she whispered frantically. The word rang ominously in her ears, while her breasts endured a strange, tingling flush. "What ritual?"

"Our mating ritual. One that's more binding than any paper or civilized law."

"This is insane." Diedre pressed as close to the

rocks as she could, drawing away from him to break the hypnotic stroke of his fingertips. Sterling countered with a more insistent pressure. "It's the wine," she said urgently. "The island. You don't know what you're doing."

"You're wrong. I know exactly what I'm doing." He pulled her roughly against him, then stripped off her top. "It's you. It's me. And it's *now*."

Before she could utter another entreaty, he backed her firmly against the rocks.

"Don't ever run from me again," he commanded. "A woman does not run from her mate."

"I am not your mate."

"You *are* my mate." He laid an ungentle claim on her heaving breasts. "It's past time you started acting like it."

"I can't," she whimpered. "Not this way."

"Oh yes, *this* way. And every other way you can possibly imagine." His mouth replaced his hand, and he sucked on her breast with a searing, greedy hunger.

Diedre's head fell back against the rocks. Her body went limp, and she braced herself to succumb to the inevitable.

She expected ravishing, and she got it. What she didn't expect was the deep, coiling heat that pulsed outward from her core and peaked at the tip of her nipple. While his tongue and lips and teeth continued their voracious plunder, his fingers worked the other bud until it was achingly distended.

She couldn't fight him. She slumped against the rock, and closing her eyes, she gave in to his masterful handling . . . and to the siren call of unleashed sexual need.

Perhaps he sensed her relinquishment. Perhaps he was only blinded by his all-consuming quest to claim his right. But his mouth moved upward and captured her lips, while his hands lowered and spread over her belly.

She accepted his hard, demanding kiss. She succumbed to his expert fondling. Indeed, she realized through the haze of riotous sensation, Sterling most definitely knew what he was doing.

The tide turned.

Acceptance became necessity. Necessity became demand. Arching into him, she returned his kiss and asked for more. Her hands no longer thrust against his chest, but matched his stroke for stroke until she was the one aggressively dictating the ritual call to mate.

"That's better," he said against her mouth. "Tell me you want this."

"I want this." Her fingers clenched his chest hair, then worked their way down.

"You want me. You want *us*."

"Yes." She pressed her fingertip into his navel. His answer wasn't a word but a pleased, seductive growl. The arousing, animalistic reply reverberated in her ears as he grasped her hands and placed them over the pelt hugging her hips.

"You want us? Then take them off."

She felt a quickening thrill. But before she could give in, her earlier fear clawed at her again with its taloned grip.

"I can't take you," she said in a tremulous voice.

"What makes you so sure?"

She drew in a shaky breath. "I . . . I saw you while you were asleep."

"And so you ran. That was folly, Diedre. You have to endure some pain before you can take the ultimate pleasure."

"The pleasure can't be worth it."

"I'll make the pleasure worth it. Before we're through, you'll wonder why you ever tried to escape."

"I can't take you," she insisted, fighting the urge to renew her struggles. "I *can't*."

"You can. And you will."

And then he was no longer kissing her mouth. He was nipping her neck, thrusting his tongue in the hollow where the runaway beat of her heart pulsed. He moved down until his teeth grazed her breasts, then forged a slow path to her navel. He bathed her abdomen, took love bites, and proceeded to spend too much time learning the inside of her thighs.

She was trembling, ready to fall, when he pushed aside the hem of her shorts and found her moist heat.

Diedre reared back, gripping his head, unprepared for the acute sensation. Why had she run? Why had she been afraid to accept such ecstatic torture as this?

She shook. She moaned. He stabbed her repeatedly with his tongue, then gently suckled her most sensitive point. It went on for an eternity; it went on not nearly long enough. She screamed his name, and she grasped for something, anything, to fill the aching, empty void within her.

Something did. His fingers worked against the barrier, and then he was filling her, but not enough. He was reaching, but not far enough. No, he didn't ease her poignant pain, but instead heightened it until it was unbearable.

"Oh God!" she shrieked. She burrowed her fingers into his hair and thrust his head back. He gazed up at her, and she saw something she'd never seen before—a stark, carnal, soulful look that was everything she could feel unfurling inside itself.

His fingers remained inside her while he continued to stroke her cleft with his thumb.

"You will take me," he said. A gritty certainty edged his tone. "You'll take me and ask for more."

She was wild. She was past any coherent thought.

Hurriedly, she stripped off the shorts, feeling no modesty or shame.

"More," she demanded. "Give me more."

His gaze fixed on her nudity. His eyes narrowed to a slit, and he suddenly grabbed her by the wrist and whipped her down to the ground. Her back was cushioned by soft grass, and she stared up at the sky. Sterling's face filled her vision. His expression was controlled, purposeful, intense.

"You'll never say I forced you. If you want more then you take off what I've got on."

Her teeth-shortened nails streaked down his chest until she found the loose leather string riding low on his hips. She tugged it free, eager for the fulfillment of his promise.

Diedre hooked her fingers into his shorts and thrust them down as far as she could.

"Please, Sterling. Get rid of it."

He obliged her, impatiently peeling and kicking off his clothes. She reached for the epitome of his strength. Closing her fingers around it, she began to pump. Air escaped raggedly through his flattened lips. His eyes went from slitted to closed. His expression neared agony.

"Now," she whispered. "Now."

"I say we take it slow. I've waited. I've chased. It's turned me inside out and left me without a stitch of control. For your sake, Diedre darlin', I'm giving you a taste of what you've dished out."

"No!"

"It's for the best. Trust me. I don't want to hurt you any more than I have to." He removed her hand with an iron grip.

With thumb and forefinger Sterling shut her eyes. She could feel him shake as he held her face with his palms. He stroked her from her head to her feet, murmuring endearments between cooing sounds.

She was melting into the grass beneath, dissolving into a pool of languorous liquid sensation.

The sudden slide of his fingers against and into her wetness was an electric, vivid contrast to the dream state of her senses. She cried out, and his mouth settled over hers to tease, to feast, to torment, until she was pleading for his mercy.

Teetering on the brink of a great unknown, Diedre clung to him, and a shuddering gap seemed to open between tactile thrust and retreat.

Then he was on top of her, probing her entry with his bluntness.

"You are my mate. Say it and I'll give you what you were running from. What you'll never run from again."

"I am your mate." Her spine arched into a bow, lifting her off the ground. Were her eyes as wild as his? And was this she bucking against him as he began to sink into her until her ungiving maidenhead stopped him? She didn't know. All she knew was that he had done this to her, and he must fill the void to assuage the terrible hurt.

"I love you, Diedre. If I could, I'd save you from this."

They were the last words she heard before he suddenly jerked his hips forward, planting himself deeper than deep. She felt the tearing as she took his body's offering. What was this rippling ecstasy shaking her to the quick? What was this sharp, caustic bite?

It was pleasure beyond her wildest dreams. It was pain beyond endurance. The pleasure peaked, and made her scream his name. Then it receded to a slow, lapping wave at low tide.

The pain, however, did not immediately abate.

Diedre stared into his pleased, knowing gaze, one reflecting the direness of his unslaked hunger. He was absolutely still, and seemed hard-pressed to remain that way.

"You're hurting me," she said, gasping. "Please, Sterling. Take yourself out. Get off."

"It's too late for that," he said in a tight voice. "Try to relax, darlin'. The best has yet to come."

She could feel him touching her womb; she could feel him pulse. Her tender, most vulnerable flesh stung while it stretched, but not quite enough.

He pulled back, then sank down again. Diedre pushed his chest with her hands.

"Stop! Stop, damn you! Get off me. Get—"

Sterling grasped her wrists and pinned them above her head. His powerful body subdued her struggles and rendered her helpless.

"Diedre, remember what I taught you. Be brave. Confront the challenge. You've always trusted me before, so don't stop now. Relax," he soothed. "Relax. Feel the earth's strength. Feel mine."

"But your strength hurts." Even as she said it, she could feel the give of her muscles, the pain turning to something closer to discomfort.

"I give you my love, Diedre. And I promise never to hurt you again. If you trust me, you'll believe that's true."

She began to accept the fullness better. Her trust in him was implicit, and she willed her taut muscles to slacken.

"I believe you," she said softly.

"But do you love me? More than anything, that's what I need to know."

He released her wrists, and she lifted her hands to cup his face. She felt her heart swell to overflowing. To keep her love to herself would be more painful than what her body had just endured.

"I do love you, Sterling Jakes. I love you more than anything or anyone. I'll give you whatever it is you need. Go ahead, take it. Take me. You *are* my mate, and I won't fight you anymore."

He shook his head, and his lips curled into a slow, sensual smile.

"Tell me, darlin', do you really think I'd take anything from you without giving it back just as good or, if I was able to, even better?"

She answered him with the offering of her lips. They shared a kiss that sealed their vows of boundless and untamed love.

"Lesson," he said quietly. "The senses. We begin with . . . touch." He guided her hand to the place of their intimate joining.

Diedre drew in a quick breath.

"Tell me what you feel," he gently commanded.

"I feel . . . us. We are one."

"That we are." He lifted her hand and brought it close to their faces. "And scent?"

Her nostrils seemed to quiver, inhaling the musk scent from their mingled bodies.

"I smell . . . lovers. Heat."

"Now look. You might be surprised."

Diedre's gaze followed the path of his. The sight of their mating was stunning. He rose, then slowly descended. She was no longer hurting, but rather in awe.

"We're beautiful together," she breathed.

"We make a perfect fit, Diedre. In more ways than I ever dreamed possible."

He was smiling as she drew his head down, and their mouths met in a gentle, then increasingly passionate kiss.

When he began to move carefully inside her, she was astonished to feel her body give, accept, and then reclaim him. Her eagerness mounted with each sleek thrust, and once she began to move, to match his steady tempo, he grasped her hips and tilted her higher. His thrusts became shallower and she found she missed feeling all of him.

"All the way," she pleaded. "Give me the light. Give me you."

"I'm all yours," he vowed. "Just as you're mine."

Their coupling entered a new dimension. He did not stroke. He did not woo. What he did do was give her a tattoo of concentrated energy as indelible as needled ink.

It was the darkness she had feared. It was the blinding light she had glimpsed, then shrunk from. Diedre knew she would never shrink again.

She hailed his masterful strength, and he paid tribute to her pagan majesty. Purr met growl and crescendoed into a symphony of unbridled, tribal wails. They wrestled; they tangled. They claimed the earth and each other with a ripping force that matched the storm's.

Then it was just the two of them with no history but the one they were creating. They crested on a dizzying cusp. Their mutual cries of ecstasy were primal and incoherent.

It was a language only lovers embracing the grand passion could speak.

Twelve

"My, oh my, if it isn't Aphrodite herself." Sterling let go a catcall. From his vantage point at the uppermost ledge of the bluff sheltering the lagoon, he could see Diedre emerge naked from the water, then wring her hair.

He watched as she stretched languorously, crystal-clear rivulets streaming down her sleek and supple muscles and inviting him for a closer inspection. Not that he didn't already have intimate knowledge of each crevice and swell. Their lovemaking over the past month had been frequent and vigorous and lush. What they shared in those and other moments was passion and companionship that went beyond his comprehension and far surpassed his previous experience.

His only regret was the precautionary withdrawal. Except for that blinding, soul-shattering first coupling when he couldn't have left her if his life had depended on it, he had done what he could to protect her from pregnancy. Children were a luxury they couldn't afford. The repercussions could be staggering.

But for now they were safe. Her menses last week had confirmed it.

Sterling stroked his newly trimmed beard, grimacing when he hit a nick. What he went through for the sake of being attractive. Hell, he'd nearly sliced his own throat with his knife! He glanced from Diedre to the sky and the sun's position. Maybe a little past two. Plenty of time to bed his woman before they had to grab their spears and lance the evening's meal.

Sterling's gaze suddenly fixed on a long vine that was attached to a branch of the tree right above his head. The vine seemed to go on forever, past his feet and all the way down the bluff.

An idea took hold. Next to John Wayne, his boyhood idol had been Johnny Weissmuller. He'd spent hours glued in front of the tube, pretending he was "Me, Tarzan."

"Well, what d'ya know? . . ." Sterling mused aloud. This was his chance to bring to life his fantasy. So what if Cheetah was on vacation? Jane was barely covered by the outfit she'd just shimmied into.

He made sure Diedre was busy combing her hair before he edged forward and grabbed the vine. It was so thick that his fingers, large as they were, didn't wrap around it completely. A good sign that it should be strong enough to take their combined weight.

Sterling gave it a trial yank. He felt a slight resistance before it gave. He'd been afraid it rooted into the crevices in the rocks, but they were shallow and easily pulled free.

Keeping a close eye on Diedre, he began to tug the vine up. She stopped combing and looked at it curiously. He stopped and flattened himself against the ground.

Diedre apparently saw nothing suspicious about the vine, for she went back to her personal toilette. He redoubled his efforts. He didn't want her to get away before he could enact his fantasy.

Sterling silently whooped once he pulled the end to the top. Vine in hand, he quickly headed for the tree and climbed up to a high limb. A quick look assured him the vine's hold on the tree was firm.

He made a trial swing, testing for strength. It worked! He began to hoist the vine, calculating the length he needed to sweep out and grab his target.

It was a clear shot. Diedre was standing just right, with nothing between them but a fifty-foot drop. Maybe he should give her just a teeny warning.

Sterling pounded his chest and let out a familiar cry.

"Ah-ahah . . . ah-ah . . . ahaha-ah!"

She looked. Once more he thumped his chest with both fists and flew from the tree. The clear water beckoned, and so did his mate, her mouth opened in a big *O*, her arms stretched wide.

"Sterling!" she shrieked, as he swooped past and grabbed her by the waist. She latched on to his shoulders for dear life, and they sailed together into the wild blue yonder for a moment that seemed endless and was sheer ecstasy. He would remember it forever, a beloved memory sealed in a seamless bubble.

He let go and they dropped to the water, all the way to the bottom. He touched the gravelly sand and claimed her lips for a kiss. They exchanged a breath between their mouths before grudgingly giving in to gravity and ascending, their limbs tangling.

They emerged, still kissing.

"What did you think you were doing?" She laughed and rubbed her dark, freckled wet nose against his.

"Gave you a thrill, huh?"

"It was . . . fantastic!" Water from Diedre's spiky lashes dropped onto her high cheekbones, and he sipped them. "At least it was terrific after my heart started beating again."

"Are you up for an encore? We could do it from the top of the tree together."

"No thanks, ape man. I've hit my quota of excitement for the day. Make that for the year."

"Sure about that?" He ducked beneath the surface and hiked up her top. Her breasts bobbed, and he fitted his lips over one of them.

She was quick to thrust into him, squirming to secure a better hold. He held his breath, and her breast in his mouth, until she yanked at his hair, pulling him up.

"You called?" he said, inhaling fresh air, fresh *her*.

Diedre broke free. "Last one to the shore . . . gets on top!"

Sterling chuckled, deliberately giving her the lead.

By the time he waded to the shallow end, she was nude and waiting. He made quick work of his shorts and snuggled into her waiting warmth.

"You're a wanton woman," he murmured huskily, then set about making her even more wanton than she already was.

"But *you*, Sterling Jakes, need such a woman to satisfy the man." Using a ninjutsu maneuver, she wasted no time changing places.

"Not fair," he growled. "You forgot the rules of the game."

"Oh, I didn't forget." She settled herself deeper and began to ride his hips. "I simply decided to expand them."

"Then you won't mind if I expand them a little more." He sat up, and they met face to face.

"You are my mate," she whispered. "You are my one and only love."

"And you are my wife. All we miss are the papers."

"To hell with the papers. Bind me with this."

He did. They merged so completely, the papers would have been torched, rendered to a heap of smoldering ash.

• • •

As Diedre and Sterling worked side by side, cleaning up after the evening's meal, she sang an old lover's melody.

"You've been singing a lot lately," he said, throwing dirty water out the cave's mouth. "Do you sing when you're happy?"

"Now I do. I used to sing when I was sad. At my parents' house I'd curl into the little window seat in my bedroom and sing a lullaby. When I was through feeling sorry for myself, I'd pick up a book and read. That always made me happy." She laughed and stoked the fire before motioning him over to their bed. "At least it made me happy until one of my parents caught me under the covers with a flashlight when I was supposed to be asleep."

"You miss your books, don't you?" Sterling sat behind her and began his nightly ritual of combing one hundred strokes through her hair. "I wish I could give you a whole library of them."

"That's okay. I'd take you over a library any day."

Lifting the flaxen strands, he pressed a kiss to her nape. "Why were you sad?"

Diedre thought back to a time that seemed so long ago.

"I probably didn't have a right to be," she finally said. "I was spoiled with material possessions. But I never really felt . . . loved—until I met you. When I was small and even when I left home, I thought it was my fault, that I was unlovable."

"Definitely a misconception on your part, darlin'."

"I've come to realize that." She sighed and nuzzled in for a closer fit of neck to mouth. "Being here's given me the distance to see that they did love me in the only way they knew how. I used to resent them, but not anymore. Sometimes I even feel sorry for . . . Mother and Father."

The names felt strange to speak, their titles as formal as her parents. She knew if she and Sterling ever had children, they would be just Mom and Dad, maybe even Mommy and Daddy.

"Do you feel sorry for them because they probably assume you're dead? I don't know about you, but it gives me a queer feeling to think our families may have already had funerals for us."

"Brrrr." Diedre shivered. "I hadn't thought of that, but you're probably right. Hey, I wonder what they said about us? Nothing bad, I bet."

"Yeah, wouldn't that be a kick? Kind of like everyone praising Tom Sawyer while his old aunt blew her honker to kingdom come."

"Do you think they had a military service for you?"

"Dad probably saw to that. I don't doubt he put on his old Korean War uniform and arranged a twenty-one-gun salute. Now Mom, she'd have on her Sunday best." Sterling's voice went husky; Diedre could feel his terrible sadness. "That's my worst regret about this whole thing. Not being marooned here, because I'm perfectly content to spend my life this way with you. But I wish somehow I could let them know we're all right. It's torn my mother up, I'm sure. Sometimes I even dream I can hear her crying."

Had her own mother cried as many tears? Diedre wondered. She'd rarely seen her cry, only a few times at the opera. The old feeling of bitter disappointment struck a tender nerve.

"I have a hard time imagining my mother like that, or my father. They probably held an elegant gathering in my honor. Father would have the men join him in his study for a toast to my memory. Mother would have spent the morning having her hair done and making sure her manicure was just right." Diedre stared at her own short nails. They were clean but bitten down close to the quick.

"Would she and the ladies join the men?"

"Hardly. They'd be talking opera and how promising I was. Of course, no one would mention the fact that I didn't have what it takes."

"You've got what it takes," he said. His anger was close to the surface; she heard it thread through his voice and in the sudden tug of the comb he plied through her hair.

"I have what it takes here," she said. "But not for professional opera. That's a sore point I'm not sure I'll ever get past."

"You were that disappointed? You never said so before."

"It wasn't my disappointment. It was Mother's. First I tried." Diedre could feel the sting of tears, and she blinked them away. "I tried so hard. Not for me, but just hoping I could please her enough to make her—"

"Love you?"

She nodded. "But then I quit trying. I was tired of beating my head against a wall and practicing music I didn't even want to sing. So then I started to resent her—and her music."

"Her music but not yours?"

"Yes." She sighed. "I guess it was sad, really. You see, Mother had a promising career just as her mother did. The way you have three generations of military on your father's side, we had three on my mother's, but it was opera. *Opera.* From the time I was born, that's all I ever heard. The word's enough to make me sick."

"Now it comes together." Sterling set aside the comb and began to braid her hair. "She lost her dream, so she wanted to live it through you."

"That's the tall and short of it."

"But why did she give it up?"

"Simple. The same reason her mother did. They married wealthy, overbearing men who thought they should devote their lives to hostessing and indulging a man's career."

"That kind of mentality is pretty archaic, if you ask me. And that's a judgment coming from another overbearing man."

"Overbearing?" She chuckled and swatted his hand as it groped around to squeeze a breast. "I think that's a fair description. But you left out your more persuasive charms. They have a way of making me overlook the beast you can be."

"Grrr." Sterling pushed her to the ground and hunkered over her on all fours. "I'll give you the beast. He's straining to get out and stroke you."

"Not so fast." Diedre shoved him off and giggled as she toyed with the string at his hips. "I want to hear about your mom's side of the family. Everything you've told me seems to be about the men."

"Sorry. Grandmother died before I was born. Grand-daddy's still fishin'."

"A fisherman?"

"Bona fide. Used to take me out on his boat. We'd oyster, set crab traps, go shrimping. I never was really good at those things, not like him, but he spent hours telling me fisherman tales. He's no different from a lot of seamen. Very superstitious about doing things that are lucky and not doing things that are unlucky."

"Like what?"

"Let's see. I always had to board on left foot first. Sneezes had to go left too. Couldn't whistle. We never got on a ship with a name ending in the letter a, because it was marked for doom. He even had a silver sixpence built into his boat's mast to protect him from storms."

"You're kidding! That's wild."

"He's still kickin', so it must work for him."

"But surely *you* don't believe any of that hooey."

Diedre considered the way he pursed his lips and his brows drew together. "Do you?"

"Maybe a little. Could be he just scared the dickens out of me with all his ghost-ship stories."

"Ghost stories? I never could stand to listen to those things. They give me the willies."

"Do they make you shudder and moan?"

"I'll say."

"Do they make you want to hide under the covers and crawl all over the person beside you to get safe?"

She nodded, already feeling a shudder roll up her spine.

"Then I've got a great one."

"No, Sterling. Don't tell me. I don't want to hear it." She clamped her hands over her ears.

"Ooooh . . . ooooh . . . oooooh!" he intoned in a ghostly chant.

"Stop it!" Diedre gave him an elbow and grabbed the soft fur coverlet he'd pieced together with strips of rawhide, then huddled underneath.

"Oh come on, darlin'. Be a sport. It's just an old sea tale. Since you don't believe in all that mumbo jumbo, you know it's not true."

She peered out and knew she was hooked as soon as she saw his boyish grin.

"Okay." She sighed. "You're going to tell me anyway, so I might as well give in."

Sterling stretched, settling in for his story, one she was sure would give her a case of the creeps. She scooted closer and wished the fire cast more light. Shadows played across the cave, taking on ominous shapes reminiscent of the bogeyman of her childhood's imagination.

"It begins with a legend," he said quietly. "The graveyard of lost ships in the sea of fear."

"I don't like the place already."

"But, Diedre, we're in it. Or at least very close by."

"What?" she squeaked.

"That's right. The Sargasso Sea. Between the West Indies and the Azores. Part of the Devil's Triangle lies in that sea, and it's a place where ships and planes go down, down, down. Never to be seen again."

"Tell me about it," she muttered wryly.

"Oh, I will. I'll tell you about the derelict ships that disappear, then reappear to haunt the place that took them to their death." His voice lowered to an ominous, hypnotic tone. "Seaweed is all around, and the water and air are too still. Yachts, pirate vessels, and Spanish galleons all share the same doom. They're caught in the Devil's lair to languish forever, and sailors stalk the ships as the living dead.

"Oh yes, few have escaped to tell the tale. But they share a terrible fate, unable to flee from the Grim Reaper's hooded face. They become mad, insane. They rant about the chanting voices they can't get out of their heads. They can smell nothing but brine and decay. And some have even put their own eyes out, trying to escape from the vision of skeletons manning the haunted boats and grabbing at them with gnarled hands as their bones clank and grind together."

Diedre's eyes were as big as saucers. "Thanks, Sterling, I really needed to hear that. Now I'm not going fishing tomorrow. Maybe I won't ever go again."

"Oh, sure you will. You'll just be looking over your shoulder for a black sail and a flag with a skull and crossbones."

She shifted, feeling uneasy. A lot of strange things did happen in this area, and she couldn't help but wonder if Sterling's story mixed a little fact with fiction.

"Is it true? About the seaweed and the still water being a trap?"

"Yeah, it is. Even Columbus wrote about this place. Of course, nowadays, with boats being powered by motors instead of sails and a good wind, it's not so dangerous."

"But the old ships?"

"I haven't seen any out haunting lately, but barnacles could grow on them and make them look scary. And I do imagine if a crew was stranded long enough, their skeletons would be lying around."

"Wouldn't they jump ship?"

"Not as long as they had food and drinking water. The sea's certainly no better bargain. Maybe that's why I'm mystified by boats being found with food still left but no people and no clues as to where they'd vanished."

Diedre frowned. It was a lot to swallow. Then again, their own experience wasn't exactly what most people would easily believe. "You mean that's actually happened?"

"Yep," he said. "Many times, and even in recent years. The Coast Guard doesn't like to talk about it because there's no logical explanation."

Diedre glanced at the flickering flames. The walls seemed to shift and change, giving her pause. Maybe the bogeyman didn't reserve his visits for children, since he seemed oblivious to the fact she'd outgrown him.

"Don't tell me anymore ghost-ship stories," she said. "I've heard all I want to hear."

"Okay. Then I'll tell you a real one about the *Ellen Austin* in 1881."

"I won't listen unless you crawl under the covers."

Sterling chuckled while he happily obliged. Wrapping her braid around his neck, he picked up where he'd left off.

"She was an American schooner out for a cruise. She came upon a ship much like herself. The other vessel was shipshape but with no signs of life, and the captain of the *Ellen Austin* decided he'd bagged quite a prize. So he put some of his men aboard, ready to take her home. But a squall came up, and they broke contact. Two days later he found her again. The ship was still good, but the men had vanished. As you might guess, the other sailors— being superstitious, of course—didn't want to test their luck."

"So they left it alone?"

"No, the captain bribed some more guys to board it."

"Maybe they had some of your homemade wine." She laughed and rolled her eyes at the vat.

"Lord, that would've put an end to them. God knows the stuff practically put an end to me." He took a love bite from her neck. "Anyway, another squall came up. The vessel and the crew of the jinxed ship were never seen again."

"That's even creepier than your ghost story."

"Is it? I haven't heard you moan or felt you shudder yet, though you're doing a good job of crawling all over me."

"Mmm . . . Then why don't you unfurl my sails and see what you find?"

"I know what I'll find. A treasure better than anything on a Spanish galleon." His hand glided over her, ridding her of the clothes. "You know, darlin', there's a romance between men and the ocean. They affectionately call their vessels *she*." He tugged and sipped at her nipple with his lips. "And the nude body of a woman on the masthead works a special magic, her bosom swelling out in search of luck and fertility from the sea. The boat slices through the waves, going up and down. Much the same way we ride together."

She succumbed to his gentle persuasion, her thighs parting to greet his questing touch.

"Ride me," she whispered.

He did. He rode her to the ends of the earth, and she rode him back. They were ships that were far from lost, finding a singular path only to collide and share the sweetest death, drowning in a pool of liquid ecstasy.

As they lay replete in each other's arms, Sterling stared up at the shadow play on the cave's ceiling.

"What are you thinking of?" Diedre stroked her hand across the hair and cooling moisture on his chest.

"Just an old poem my grandfather taught me."

"Share it with me?"

He tightened his hold and whispered:

> "The spectre ship in vivid glympsing light,
> Glares balefully on the shuddering watch at night,
> She haunts the sea where the unwary have trod,
> Unblest by man or God."

Thirteen

Diedre drained a large conch shell the tide had washed up and put her ear to the curved opening. Listening to the sound of waves echoing through the hollow chambers, she let the rushing rhythm lull her senses. It was a soothing contrast to the raging storm that had swept through yesterday. She wondered if they were in for another one. The sky was overcast, and the wind vacillated between calm and frenzied, resulting in a curious mixture of warm and cool air.

"Sterling," she called. "Look. Another shell for my collection."

Sterling glanced up from his task and smiled. He was sorting through the debris the storm had cast ashore, searching for anything of use.

"You're doing better than I am," he said. "So far I've found seaweed, dead fish, and—ah, what have we here?" He studied a ripped piece of mangled fabric. "Wonder where this came from? It's thick, like canvas."

"Maybe a sailboat got caught in the storm."

"Maybe, but judging from the condition of this, I'd

guess it's a remnant from a sail that was torn up a long time ago."

Sterling tossed it aside and got up. He pulled Diedre into his arms and said, "Will you still love me when I'm an old remnant hobbling around the cave and you're still a young woman scaling trees? There's more than a little age difference between us."

"I love you now, and I'll love you then." She dropped the shell and ran her hands over the hair dusting his chest. "Speaking of age differences, sometimes I can't believe that when you were already grown and in the Berets, I was barely eight. While I was reading Nancy Drew, you were probably carousing in bars."

"I did my share of carousing."

"Did you pick up any women along the way?"

"On occasion."

She was terribly jealous. "How many? One, two, a harem?"

"Would it make you jealous if I said dozens?"

"Pea green."

"Then I had tons of women fighting over me. Mauling each other to see who could get to me first."

"Liar!" she said, though in truth she didn't doubt his claim. Diedre punched him playfully in the stomach.

"It's true. But I told them I was saving myself for an eight-year-old who liked to read books." He flirted with her lips, but Diedre stopped the kiss.

"There were a lot of women, weren't there, Sterling?"

"A few."

"Any who tempted you to walk down the aisle again?"

He studied her face while he seemed deep in some internal debate. Sterling opened his mouth, then shut it. His reaction was unexpected; it left her with the suspicion he was keeping something from her.

Another woman, to be exact. Whoever she was, Diedre didn't like her.

"Sterling?" she prompted. "Who was she?"

"No one who matters anymore, Diedre. You're my other half, and I'm bound to you. For now, let's leave it at that. I don't want to spoil the day by talking about old relationships when ours is the only one that counts." He hugged her tightly and kissed her before she could continue probing. "I never really loved another woman, and there's no room left in my heart or in my bed for anyone but you."

She fought the urge to dig for more information, though hearing about old flames would probably hurt and stoke her unfounded jealousy. Sterling was hers, and she didn't like to think of his being with another, even before they had met.

"Oh well." She sighed, "I don't guess that's too hard a promise to keep as long as we're stranded here."

"It's a promise I'll never break, no matter where in the world we live. You'd better never make the mistake of forgetting that, woman. Especially since I expect an equal measure of devotion and fidelity from my mate. I could get pretty ugly if my territory was infringed upon."

"Could you? I might be tempted to find out just how possessive you could get."

"How about a little demo right now? Just to keep you honest, I'll be generous with my warning." He had her over his knee in a millisecond. Diedre squealed and squirmed while he pushed up the hem of her shorts and playfully swatted her pert rear.

"Stop!" she shrieked, laughing. "I was kidding."

"In that case, I'll kiss it and make it better."

He made good on his promise, then turned her around until she sat on his lap. Her arms were around his neck, and they were rubbing noses when she glanced out to the sea.

Her gaze settled on a low fog rolling off the horizon.

Sterling ceased playing and he, too, stared at the queer cloud. A large, dark, hulking object emerged. Diedre had learned to take many strange things for granted in these parts, but this was stranger than usual.

"Sterling, is that what I think it is?"

"Well, I'll be," he said. "Looks like an old ship."

"Or what's left of one." They got to their feet without taking their eyes off the battered vessel. "How do you think it got here?"

"The storm must've pushed it this way. Reminds me of a restored clipper I saw in Boston Harbor from the Tea Party days, though this one's beyond help. Could be that piece of canvas came from the thing." Sterling squinted his eyes, concentrating on the vessel. "You stay here. I'm swimming out to look it over."

Diedre clutched his arm. She couldn't explain it, but an uneasy sensation churned in the pit of her stomach. The clipper struck her as somehow repulsive. Perhaps it was the way it reminded her of an insect. The hull resembled a roach's carcass, with flapping, chewed-up wings that passed themselves off as tattered sails and were attached to spindly mast poles that pricked the sky like seeking antennae.

"Don't go," she said.

"Why not? There might be something on board we could use."

"What? It looks like vultures have picked it clean."

"There's no telling for certain unless I check it out."

Sterling started for the water, and she was right on his heels.

"And where do you think you're going?" he demanded.

"I'm not letting you swim out there alone and leave me stranded here. I can't explain it, but I just don't have a good feeling about this."

"For heaven's sake, Diedre, you're being ridiculous."

"But the story you told me, about the death ships, about them being here and—"

"That's just an old legend."

"Legends can be true, can't they? And the way that boat looks, the barnacles, the rotten wood, the—"

"Skeletons grinding their bones? Come on, Diedre, I already told you barnacles grow on derelict ships, and they get covered with seaweed. Even if there are skeletons lying around, they're just people who got trapped on board and starved."

"But look at the sky, Sterling. A storm could come up before you make it back, and it might take you out with the ship."

"I'll jump, okay? Now let me get out there in case you're right. I don't want to lose it before I have a chance to inspect it."

"But what about sharks?"

"The ship's close, and I'll be careful to stroke quietly so I won't catch their attention."

Diedre knew his mind was made up, and that was that. She also knew she wasn't about to stay put while Sterling satisfied his curiosity. The clipper could be blown farther out to sea with him on it. Even worse, he could go down with the ship if it suddenly sank, which seemed a dangerous possibility. Come what may, she would rather share his fate than live her life without him.

"All right, go," she growled. "Do you have the knife?"

"Got it." Sterling left her with a kiss and another warning not to budge, then waded into the crystal water.

She waited until he was more than halfway, then eased into the sea, making sure he didn't notice. He swam fast and sure, and she was barely a quarter of the way when she saw him latch on to something hanging over the side of the boat. She realized it was a ladder made of rope, but even from here it looked ready to disintegrate. She hoped it would snap with his weight, and he'd be forced to turn back.

No such luck. Diedre watched him scale the side, and she ducked under the water when she saw him turn to make sure she was still on shore. She didn't have to hear his voice to guess he was spitting out enough sour words to curdle milk.

Diedre streaked through the ocean as quietly as she could while she tried not to think about sharks. Once she reached the boat, she saw Sterling glaring at her over the side.

"Dammit, Diedre. When we get back to shore, you'd better hightail it away from me. I *told* you not to follow me out here."

"Well, I'm here now, so you might as well let me help."

Sterling's vocabulary was nothing if not colorful, she thought as he growled his begrudging consent for her to climb. She didn't like the unpleasant slippery feel of the old twine in her hands. As for the ship itself, she preferred Sterling's glower to the barnacles covering the rotting wood. They resembled infected boils that snails were feeding on, and it seemed as if they were slowly devouring the ship.

Diedre grabbed Sterling's outstretched hand and gratefully accepted his assistance. The deck was splintered and warped but surprisingly solid beneath her feet.

When she gave their host a curious once-over, what she saw was a leering travesty of ancient grandeur. The clipper had been proud once. The length from bow to stern was long, but the width was modest. She gazed almost sadly at the tall masts, tilted askew with their pitiful sails that clung as tenaciously as parasites.

"Well?" he said gruffly. "Was it worth the swim?"

"Let's see." Maybe if she found something worth salvaging, Sterling wouldn't be so put out. A knife would definitely be a good bargaining tool. "Should we split up? We can finish faster that way." She glanced at the sky and the eerie tendrils of fog that couldn't seem to decide whether or not to stay. Her earlier premonition of danger intensified, and she tried unsuccessfully to ignore it.

"Fine. I'll go below while you check up here." He started for the cabin and threw over his shoulder, "Yell if the fog thickens or if the wind picks up."

"Aye-aye, Captain." As soon as he was gone, Diedre cautiously picked her way around broken boards, dead birds, and empty casks until she discovered a bell mounted near the helm. Before she touched it, it clanged once, then twice.

Odd, she thought. At the moment, the wind wasn't strong enough to swing a heavy, rusted bell.

Her apprehension climbed another notch, and she left the bell alone. She was finishing this search as soon as possible. Even now she could feel the boat shifting with a creak and a sway. More than anything she wanted them to go home and forget this scavenger hunt.

Moving hastily down the clipper's length, she discovered an unexpected find. A massive chest, similar to what she imagined a pirate would stash his treasure in. The lid was curved, the decayed wood held together by several metal strips.

Could there be jewels inside? Not that they could do much with them on the island. But what if there was a dagger? Ah, there was a thought. A dagger embellished with rubies and emeralds, fit for her swarthy mate.

She noticed the wind seemed to have gained a little speed. A quick glance to the island assured her they were drifting out to sea. She would give the chest a minute, maybe two, and then they'd be on their way.

Quickly, she twisted and turned the brittle lock until it fell open. Diedre tried to hoist the lid, but it wouldn't budge. She lost track of time and worked up a sweat as she doubled her effort.

The wind gained momentum just as she gave a final tug.

The top suddenly flew back on its rusted hinges. She stared aghast while her vocal chords strangled on a scream. Her gaze refused to jerk away, remaining fixed in horrified fascination on the skeletal remains inside the chest.

A skull was on top, its empty sockets staring back at her. She wondered with morbid curiosity what kind of sick mind was behind locking another person in a chest to die. Or could it be that the chest was used as a casket that had never made it home? Or had someone hidden in there, only to find a fate worse than what he or she had been trying to escape from?

Diedre stumbled back and frantically headed for the cabin. The wind began to howl, blowing the gathering fog about her head and legs so that she felt as though she were in a scene from a gothic novel.

"Sterling!" she shrieked. "Sterling!"

He was there before she could scream his name again.

"The ch-chest," she stammered between chattering teeth. "Bones. Skeleton. In the chest."

He looked in the direction her shaking finger pointed, then around at the swirling mist.

"Tell me about it on shore. We've got to get out of here before the wind gets any worse. It could pass, but we can't take any chances, and the ship's starting to move too fast."

He grasped her by the arm, and she wondered if it was the shock of her discovery that was causing time to stretch like elastic. For a moment her vision blurred, but then she realized it was the fog that was making everything look hazy.

"Jump!" he commanded, picking her up and hoisting her over the side.

Diedre hit the bracing water and emerged just in time to see Sterling gain his footing on the rail.

"Sterling! Quick!"

Her words were blown away by a violent gust of wind. The mast and sails went wild beneath the onslaught, like a carnival ride gone mad, while Sterling battled the force of the wind pushing him back.

His reflexes were quick, and he regained his footing. Just as he arched to dive, a mast was ripped from its fragile hold and hurtled by him, striking his skull. She watched in speechless horror as the blow sent him somersaulting through the air and into the water.

She thought she screamed. She wasn't sure. Her hands were stroking through the water, but she couldn't feel them. She couldn't feel anything but shock and the frantic compulsion to get to his limp body floating on the foam. She couldn't hear anything but her swishing heartbeat—and another sound. A bell perhaps. Striking twice.

When she reached him, he was chanting, "I feel no pain. I feel no pain."

He continued reciting the self-hypnotic incantation as she treaded water and examined his injuries as best she could. Blood oozed between her fingers when she touched the dime-sized puncture behind his ear. A long slash extended from just below his temple to his cheek.

"The shore," she said urgently. She felt him grasp at her waist while he stroked with a single arm. Though they held each other tightly she realized she was carrying most of his weight over the waves. Their island beckoned even as her heart sank. The boat had indeed drifted; they seemed twice as far away.

The wind slowed their progress, cruelly assaulting them and taunting them with high-pitched, whistling moans.

Then she heard a splintering noise, a rumble of creaking and groaning and wood coming apart at the seams. She chanced a backward glance in time to see the ship folding in on itself. She was glad to see it meet its death, taking its secrets and mysterious bells and boxed-up skeletons along with it.

As though the wind were satisfied by the destruction, it miraculously headed out to the open sea, fog in tow. Diedre was grateful the two brutish companions took their swift leave, doubtless to raise holy hell elsewhere.

When she turned her attention back to shore, she spied a sharp fin cut in front of them and circle behind, then loop around again, only closer.

Shark!

"Smelled my blood," Sterling groaned. "I'm gone. Save yourself."

She felt him let go, and she held him tighter.

"Sterling!"

"You've got what it takes to survive. Now . . . get out . . . while it feeds. It's your only chance . . . darlin'."

The shark tightened its circle before she felt a horrifying nudge push Sterling against her side. He had taught her the pattern: They liked to play with their food before digging in.

Diedre didn't think. She acted on sheer instinct to save her other half, her reason for living.

She plunged beneath the surface and went straight for the knife. Sterling tried to push her away, but she was stronger and claimed it. She released the longest switch, its tip slicing through the water.

She thought her lungs would burst and her eyes would be blinded by the sting of salt as she desperately sought for the underside of the shark closing in on Sterling.

He's not yours, you murdering bastard, she thought. *He's mine, and I'll die before I let you have him.*

Finished with the last stalking lap, the shark skimmed the surface and speeded up, oblivious to her, its eyes only on Sterling. Diedre forgot her burning lungs. She forgot everything but the sleek white belly streaking fast with wide-open jaws and jagged teeth.

When the shark was but a few inches away, she stabbed its gullet and sliced down. "*Dead man's wish,*" she remembered Sterling say. "*Through the jugular and down to the heart.*"

She thrust deeper until her hand was inside and hitting bone. The shark whirled out in a mad, convulsive writhing, jerking her along with it in palsied outrage. Blood gushed into water, surrounding her with a sickening shade of pink.

If we both die, so be it, she thought. *I don't want to live without you, my mate, my husband.*

Diedre tore herself loose, her hand still clutching the knife in a fierce grip. She kicked and broke through the surface, gasping for air. She reached for Sterling and saw his eyes open and glazed. But he breathed. Thank God, he breathed!

She latched her arm around his neck and struck out. It was only then that she saw the swarm coming. Gray fins, too many to count, sliced near the surface to join their wounded companion.

Fourteen

"Don't swim," Sterling whispered. "Don't even . . . breathe."

"But the sharks—"

"If we move . . . they'll notice . . . us." Sterling's head lolled sideways, and she knew he was trying to keep from bleeding into the sea. Her gaze riveted to the bloodthirsty pack, she did what she could to staunch the flow with her thumb.

"But if we stay—"

"Wait," he whispered, "Wa . . ."

He didn't finish the word before his eyes drifted shut, then snapped open, but still glazed.

The stream of fins swiftly came closer, and Diedre commanded her self not to shriek in terror. Their hearing was as good as their sense of smell.

The wounded shark thrashed back and forth, a little over twelve feet behind them. The others closed in on it, and she wondered wildly if they had the capacity to feel sympathy, if they meant to tend their comrade before seeking a wrathful revenge.

And then she saw the unbelievable. The sharks circled behind them, so close she could feel the rush of plowed water. They formed a tight ring around the dying target, giving her and Sterling more precious space.

One shark finally rushed in and tore a piece out of the flailing, blind victim. The others quickly joined in, mauling and maiming in a cannibalistic attack.

"Now!" Sterling whispered sharply.

Diedre was barely aware that she moved her hand to hold him tightly by the arm. She was even less aware that she put the knife in her mouth and gripped it with her teeth before she began to swim. Adrenaline gave her the strength to cut through the waves while death nipped at her kicking feet.

"How long before they're finished?" she gasped.

"Three minutes . . . maybe."

She could feel him weakening by the second, but thank God, the shore was closer. They were thirty feet away when a prickling sensation made her look back. She saw the enemy re-form and begin to streak toward them.

Still hungry, you bastards? She wanted to cry out. *Tough luck. We're not free for lunch.*

Diedre felt her toes touch bottom. She forged ahead, the finish line in sight. Sterling was unconscious, his dead weight carried by her strength and the waves. By the time she waded to shore, she was sucking in air with great, heaving gulps. She took the knife from her mouth and flung it to land, mentally marking the spot.

When the lap of water could help her no more, she thrust her hands under his armpits and locked her fingers around his chest. She dragged him, not stopping until her quivering muscles gave way and she fell back, hitting dry sand.

She got up, her attention drawn to the retreating fins before she fixed her gaze on Sterling. Her heart squeezed tight, and tears she didn't know she was crying streamed down her face from her stricken, wide-open eyes.

Her fearless warrior, her soul's mate, lay too still. His breath was a thin whisper. And he was bleeding profusely, his life pooling vividly on the pristine beach.

"Sterling," she cried. "God help me, *what do I do?*"

Diedre bent down, her hair falling over him. She stroked her hands frantically over his face as she kissed his waxen lips. The cut gaped open, and more blood seeped out. If she didn't close his wounds, he would die, and he would die soon.

No hospital. No doctor. Only her and her too-little knowledge. Suture them? She had no needle, no thread. Let the skin heal by itself? No time, no time. Cauterize? Her stomach turned, and she nearly retched. It would take too long to gather material and start a fire.

Pack it. Wrap it tight. Where had the answer come from? She didn't know, but she thought it carried the command of his voice.

Diedre ran to fetch the knife. She seized it and immediately sliced off a long strip of fabric from her top, along with a tiny piece. Quickly going back to kneel over Sterling, she embedded the animal hide into the puncture. Shuttering her mind to queasiness, she set about examining the facial rip.

He would be scarred, but the flesh would eventually heal. It was the bleeding she had to fight; infection would be her next enemy. She saw that sand clung to the open wound, and she cleaned it with salt water.

Sterling flinched, and she was grateful for even that small sign of life. *Pack it.* The words again. Diedre remembered the trick of dry grass absorbing her flow.

Sprinting into the jungle, she scooped up handfuls in her shaking palms. When she returned, he was just as she'd left him, but the blood was starting to clot. She pressed the wound together, carefully packed the grass over it, then tightly wound the strip of hide around his head.

Done. Now what? The cave. But how? She couldn't carry him all that way.

Blanket, Diedre. Can haul.

Her gaze darted to his mouth. His lips were lax, so he couldn't have spoken. Why had she imagined his voice?

She ran to the cave and grabbed the quilt of tanned pelts. He was still breathing when she got back. She spread the blanket out next to him and quickly hoisted him onto it.

Sterling began to shiver, and she wrapped him up. Now how was she going to pull him? She had no rope.

A vision of Sterling lifting her into his arms and sailing through the air on a vine cut through her mind.

Her legs flew over sand and bramble until she spotted a long vine. She hacked off an ample length.

It wasn't easy, but she managed her mission. Diedre nodded in satisfaction when she finally looked at Sterling's bound form. The vine was snug around his chest and under his arms. Grabbing the long end that twisted out beneath his torso, she hoisted the vine over her shoulder and trudged doggedly ahead.

The trek was torturous. It lasted forever and demanded more strength than she possessed. And then she had none. She had only her will and her love to force her on.

Perhaps it was Sterling's own will to live and his love for her that kept him alive through the arduous trip. How long she pulled and struggled she had no idea, but the sun was dipping low by the time she reached the cave.

Diedre collapsed onto the stone floor. She ached all over and was beyond exhaustion. But she crawled to lie beside him and hugged him tight.

"Sterling," she whispered. "We're home. You're safe."

Her palms bore blisters. Her fingers were stiff yet trembling as she began to loosen the binding from his body. He was limp, and if it weren't for his shallow, erratic breathing, she would have thought him dead.

"Don't die," she pleaded, kissing his face while she cried and shook and murmured endearments.

Bracing herself, she undid the tourniquet. The grass was matted with blood, but the flow had almost stopped. Or perhaps he was running out of blood. She knew what she had to do. It was horrible, unthinkable, but necessary. If she didn't, he could lose more precious drops, and his weakened body would be wide open to infection.

The kettle held fresh water. She scrubbed her hands with soap, then gently sponged both wounds clean. Applying salve that he'd made from healing herbs and aloe was next. That done, she bent her attention to making the fire. It seemed to take forever.

And then it didn't take long enough.

The blade gleamed brightly, then turned a molten red. She could feel the sheath burn in her palm as she took halting steps toward Sterling, then dropped to her knees. Her voice a cracked whisper, she said, "God, please, just give me the strength to do what I have to do." She tenderly kissed Sterling's lips. "I love you. I love you. . . ."

Diedre applied more healing ointment before pressing the torn skin together. She sealed the puncture, then the slash, with the sizzling edge of blade. The sound, the smell, the whole horrible process of cauterization, seared through her heart as sharply as her careful strokes seared the wounds.

It was over. Diedre flung the blade aside and laid her ear over his heart.

It beat slowly and faintly, but it did beat. She stroked her hand over his body, touching him wherever she could. Shuddering sobs racked her breast, and she wept herself into a dreamless sleep.

Diedre awoke with a start. It was night. Sterling was murmuring incoherently while he twitched, ridding himself of her slight weight. Quickly, she felt his forehead.

Scalding! Infection? Or reaction to the crude operation? Both? Silently cursing herself for falling asleep, she grabbed the salve and did her best to apply it to the long, angry welt and the smaller injury. His massive body arched up, and he flung an arm out, smacking her hard on the shoulders. His eyes opened. He stared sightlessly at her face and shouted an obscenity, then slumped back to the floor and fell into a fitful sleep.

Diedre tended him through endless hours, her determination battling despair, until the morning that would not come at long last came. She'd made it through the rough night. Thank God, so had he.

His wounds were livid but hadn't festered. He was still hot, but the fever had lessened. Sterling moaned past dehydrated lips. She brought him water, dribbling it into his dry mouth. The little liquid she got down wasn't enough. *Herbs.* She needed herbs to fight the fever and any possible infection.

It tore at her heart to leave him, but she did, taking the sling and a pouch. She soon returned with what she needed. Food, in case he regained consciousness, and wild ginseng, which she brewed to make a medicinal tea.

She bathed him, applied salve, got as much tea down into him as she could. She ate sparingly of the rabbit stew she made and prayed that by tomorrow

he would be able to take a single taste of the broth.
Time rolled slowly on rusty wheels, but eventually the
next day dawned, shining and bright. Worn out from
the constant vigil, Diedre was slumped against the
wall, her chin dropped to her chest.

"Diedre?"

Her head snapped up. Had she dreamed it?

"Diedre."

Sterling had called to her! His voice was weak but
the most beloved thing she'd ever heard in her life.

"Sterling!" She ran to him, almost tripping over her
own feet and falling on top of his chest. She felt his
forehead. The fever remained, but it was low, man-
ageable.

He slowly opened his eyes while he summoned a
half-smile.

"Why aren't you sleeping with me . . . darlin'?"

Diedre began to cry. She began to laugh. And then
she bathed his face with tender kisses.

"Got one helluva headache," he muttered faintly.
"Did I tie one on last night? I oughta know better
than to drink that damn wine." He lifted his hand
and touched her face. "Got cotton mouth."

"You're thirsty!" She fetched the container of tea,
then raised his head so he could drink. Oh, the
sound of him gulping it down—how sweet, how
precious. Hours before she'd been lucky if he swallowed a few drops.

Resting his head in her lap, she stroked his hair
and realized the sealed wound was still red but no
longer angry-looking. Sterling's hand shook when he
tried to touch the healing scar. She grasped his
wrist.

"Don't touch," she said firmly. "You've been hurt."

"How bad?"

"Bad." She kissed his hand, then laid it over his
chest. "But you're healing well."

"Do I look ugly?"

"You look beautiful," she said in a choked voice.

"Well, you look like hell, darlin'. I must've put you through a lot."

"We were both put through a lot." She wondered if he'd suffered a concussion. "Do you remember anything? How you got hurt?"

"My brain's fuzzy."

She recounted their ordeal, not leaving out the rusty old bell.

"It rang twice before I touched it."

His drowsy eyes snapped open. "The wind?"

"The wind wasn't very strong at that point. I thought it rang two times again after we made it to the water. The wind could have done it then. But not the first time."

A shadowed expression passed fleetingly across his haggard features. "Had to be the wind both times."

"Sterling? Do you know anything about bells that ring by themselves?"

"Just something my granddaddy passed along. Old sailor's lore that can't hold water."

"Tell me."

"Death bell," he said quietly. "The bell that rings without human hands." They shared a small silence, each willing disbelief or a laugh of dismissal that didn't come.

Fatigue, however, did. Sterling nuzzled close to her breast, and his eyes drifted shut. "Think I'll catch a few winks."

"Sleep, darling," she murmured. "Sleep." Diedre traced his lips with her fingers and thought back to the day the storm had driven them here.

One of her first memories was of Sterling carrying her to the jungle. His words floated hauntingly around her mind, assuming a new and ominous meaning:

"Take it from an old salt, darlin'. . . . When you take a date with The Devil, it's a whole new set of rules."

Within a day he was eating, in two more he was sitting up and sharpening his blades. A week later he was practicing *katas* and getting ornery, since she insisted on doing the hunting and was still fretting over his health.

"Here, Sterling, take a sip of this fish stew." Diedre nudged his surly lips with it while he eyed the keg of wine.

"Don't want it," he said crossly.

"It does a body good," she singsonged.

"Diedre, I am not an invalid. Please quit treating me like one. It's driving me nuts."

"But you need it to regain your strength," she insisted.

Sterling grabbed her wrist and sent the broth flying.

"Wanna find out just how strong I am? Let's go to bed so you can see for yourself."

"You're not up to it," she said firmly, freeing her wrist.

"Quite the contrary, darlin'. I'm definitely up, so let's get to it. Starting right now, this savage is back on track."

Sterling clamped his mouth over hers before she could protest. To hell with her sweet little kisses, he thought. He wanted fire, he wanted passion, he wanted a woman, not a mother hen. She tried to fight him off, but he proceeded to demonstrate just how well he had recuperated. Hoisting her over his shoulder, he strode to their pallet, then deposited her on the bed. Making short work of their clothes, he ravished her mouth until she quit resisting.

"My mate," she said with a rush of emotion before stroking his back and gripping his buttocks. "I've missed you being this way. I've missed *us.* Make love to me now, then make love to me again."

His own need was too great. He was thankful Diedre was suddenly as desperate and impatient as he. They greedily took possession of each other's bodies. Sterling milked her breasts and growled a mating sound. His fingers grazed the juncture of her thighs and found her already eager and moist. She reached for him, and the contact elicited a haunting, electric thrill.

Their coupling was brief and frantic, but seared with heated devotion. They climaxed on a rippling wave, somehow bound as never before.

"I love you," she whispered, crying freely.

"Don't cry, darlin'," he said, sipping each tear. "I wasn't that bad, was I?"

"No," she said, laughing around a sob. "It's just that . . . I know I've been smothering you lately, not wanting you to do anything or even get out. But, Sterling, you don't know how much you scared me. I—I thought I'd lost you. Everytime I remember . . . God, I can't bear to think you might have died."

"Now, now," he said soothingly. "It'll take more than a scratch and a bump on the noggin to kill a tough hombre like me. You're stuck with your old man. We're together for good."

"Promise?" Her eyes were misty, her lashes wet.

"Promise." Locking their hands, he said, "See this? Diedre, it's how tight we're bound. There's something between us I can't even describe."

"I know. It's . . . strange. When I was fighting to save you, I didn't know what to do. But then I thought I heard your voice guiding me each step of the way."

"That's what I mean. We've bonded somehow.

Here." He touched his forehead to hers. "Here." His fingers made a bridge from his chest to hers, connecting both their hearts. "And definitely, here." Sterling ground his hips over hers.

"We do belong to each other," she said fervently. "It's a wonder we don't look alike."

"Never that. You're beautiful." He touched his facial scar and shook his head. "I never thought I was overly vain, but this bothers me some."

"Why? I certainly like what I see." Diedre traced the scar with her fingertip. "I think you're a gorgeous man. And you're kinder and braver than any person I've ever known."

Sterling nipped her finger. "And strong?"

"Oh yes, very strong. Apparently, you *are* up to snuff." She wrapped her arms around his neck and brought his face down for a closer inspection. "You know, I think I did a pretty darn good job with that wound. Actually, Sterling, given a little time, that scar might make you look even sexier."

"Sexier, huh?"

"Mmmm . . . definitely sexy. Females have a thing for men with a mark like that. It's . . . dangerous. Reminds a woman of a pirate."

"In that case I don't mind the scar," he said, feeling much better. "You're a good woman, Diedre. You saved me, you nursed me and took my responsibilities on your shoulders, along with your own. I want to give you something as a token of my esteem." Sterling kissed her quickly, then got up and went straight to his most prized possession.

Pressing the *manji shuriken* star blade in her hand, he said, "*Moko tora.* For you, my fierce tigress."

She stared in awe at the star and then at him.

"I am honored," she said solemnly. "I will treasure this always. But I don't know that I deserve it."

"You do. And the honor is mine to have you for my

mate. I'm giving you what the Grandmaster gave me in respect for my courage. It's only right that I pass it on." He smiled proudly and captured her lips for a sweetly fierce kiss. "You see, Diedre, you proved your spirit is worthy of the tribute. You're as brave as any warrior I've ever known."

Fifteen

They were spearing for fish when Sterling heard it. He stopped in mid-throw, tilting his ear up to tap into the distant sound.

"Sterling, look! I—"

"Shhh!" It came closer, and his gaze locked on a pinpoint dot in the sky. "Chopper," he muttered, gesturing to the far sea.

"A helicopter?" Diedre dropped her spear and squinted her eyes against the sun's glare.

"It's searching," he said. "Flying too low not to be."

He darted a gaze to Diedre when it came closer. Her face reflected . . . distress?

"What's wrong?" he said, once again focused on the small craft that unbelievably seemed to be heading their way. "You look upset."

"What if it finds us?" she said quietly.

"Then we're rescued."

"That's not what I mean. If we're found, then . . . we have to go back. To civilization, to another way of life."

"Don't you want to?" The chopper was sweeping in close, very close.

"I—I don't know." Diedre clutched his arm. "This is . . . home."

It flew directly overhead, and Sterling automatically lifted his arms, waving frantically. Diedre's hands dropped limply to her sides. He waited on edge for several seconds as the helicopter passed him. Then it reappeared, circling overhead, then hovering.

"Found us!" he whooped. Sterling grabbed Diedre to him and whirled her around.

The helicopter began to drop, and his heart raced as he watched it land. He could see a pilot giving him the thumbs-up sign, then leaning over to push out the passenger door. A small young woman alighted. Long raven hair, dark sloe eyes, and a porcelain face. She started walking their way.

Ming! Oh dear God, what . . . how . . . of all people to be here! Sterling grabbed ahold of Diedre's shoulders and jerked her around to face him.

"Listen to me, darlin'. There's something you've got to know."

"Sterling!" Ming called, quickening her steps.

"She knows you?"

"Ming," he said, wondering what in heaven's name he was going to do. His heart hammered against his ribs. His stomach churned acid.

"The girl you saved? She's beautiful, she's—"

"I don't know how to tell you this, and I need time to explain. But, Diedre, Ming's not just anyone," he said with frantic urgency in his voice.

Diedre's face went white. He could feel her begin to shake as badly as he.

"Sterling!" Ming called again, waving and coming too close too fast.

"Tell me," Diedre demanded. "Who *is* she to you?"

Sterling took a deep breath. "We're engaged."

"She's your fiancée?" Diedre stared at him, stunned, horrified. Then she flung his hands aside and gasped, "*No!*"

"I love you, Diedre. I promise—"

"Give me no promises," she cried in a voice so riddled with hurt, he physically ached. For him, for her, for their paradise lost. "Run with me," she desperately demanded.

"We can't run. Don't you understand? We can't stay here."

"She won't find us at the cave." Diedre took a halting step away. "Come with me. If you love me, you'll do it."

"I do love you. But I can't turn my back on the world."

"You filthy liar! You want to go back with her, back to the old life you had. If you didn't, you'd want to stay. Our lives belong here, not there."

"You're wrong." He reached for her. "Please, Diedre—"

Hissing, she swiped at him, her hand a vicious claw raking five stripes down his chest. Her eyes darted from him to Ming, who had stopped several yards away. Diedre hissed at him again, then bolted with Amazon speed into the haven of jungle.

"Oh God," he groaned in misery. Sterling dropped his head into his hands. A soft, gentle palm touched him.

"Sterling? What is wrong?"

He raised his face and looked at his fiancée. Where to start? How to tell her? His life here, anywhere, belonged with Diedre. Ming had to know. But he owed it to her to break the news gently.

"How did you find us?" Sterling shoved aside his acute distress while he commanded his mind to immediately form a merciful plan.

"Grandfather. He refused to believe you were dead because he still felt your ninja spirit. Many months now he has searched wide and far without stopping for rest. He will be pleased that we have found you."

"But why isn't he here? Why did he send you alone?"

Her fragile features took on a sad, mournful expression. Tears sparkled in her dark, tilted eyes.

"Grandfather is in Japan. He is very ill, Sterling. I told him I would help the pilot search since he could not." She gripped his arm in a pleading gesture. "Please, there is no time to waste. We must go quickly. If you come, perhaps you can share your strength. You are like his son, Jakes-san."

His gut twisted up tight, and his heart throbbed heavily. Loyalty. He owed it to Diedre. He owed it to the Grandmaster. Ming herself was emotionally bereft. At a time like this how could he destroy any illusions she might harbor for a happy marriage? He had to tell her, but now was not appropriate. And what of the Grandmaster, who took delight in what he thought was a perfect union? If he was near death, it would be inhumane to heap more trauma on him.

It was a rending decision, but Sterling knew there was no other way. He would have to put off telling Ming the truth. All he could do was pray that Diedre would hear him out, and have enough faith in him to wait while he worked things out in Japan.

"Okay," Sterling said slowly. "Tell you what, Ming. I have to go find my—" *Mate. Wife. Companion.* "You saw the other woman, and she's a little upset because . . . well, Diedre's attached to the island."

"She does not wish to leave?"

"No. You have to understand we spent a lot of time here. It's become . . . like home. I need to find her so we can talk about it. While I'm taking care of that, you go back and get the pilot to radio the closest landing strip. Have him give instructions to contact my folks. Hers too—right away. They can be reached at Hyannis Port in Massachusetts. Her father's name is Alexander Forsythe. They've got a private plane, and it might help if they're around when we get back."

"As you wish, Sterling." Ming bowed, then kissed him affectionately on the cheek before she left to do his bidding.

Now for the hardest part. He had to find Diedre and make things as right as he could. Would she be at the cave? He'd check there first and say his good-byes to their home. If she wasn't there, he knew where he'd find her. In her little nook, the one he had never let her know he'd found.

Diedre hugged her arms around her legs, tucked into the fetal position as she moaned her tortured animal sounds in her place. Her heart was cut so deep, she wondered why she wasn't lying in a pool of blood. Perhaps she would be lucky and die of the pain.

She knew she could never go back to the life she had once had. Her life belonged here. Was she not a huntress, a woman strong in herself and a worthy mate for the man she loved beyond human measure?

Sterling. He was hers and no other's. Ming had no right to him. The possessiveness she felt was savage, fierce. She wanted to drive a knife into Ming's heart until Ming was wounded and bleeding as badly as she.

Diedre whimpered, her dry sobs broken and wretched. Why didn't he run away with her? Didn't he know they belonged here together? But he had refused her, and she knew nothing she could say or do would make him bend. He was determined to leave, and she knew he would force her to go too.

And even if she could hide from him, would she want to live her days here alone? Her life was forged with Sterling's, and he would be gone.

Again, she saw his agonized face as he'd told her he was engaged to that . . . that . . . Ming. She couldn't stand to remember it. But her merciless mind refused to let it go. The memory of their rescue beat at her.

The helicopter. Her claw. Ming dressed in silk. Her own tanned pelts. The helicopter. Her hiss.

Diedre felt suddenly chilled. Is this what she had become? A creature no more civilized than a cat acting on instinct in the jungle? And here she lay mewling and thirsting for blood in a damp, small place she had stolen from spiders and roaches.

"Diedre!"

She heard his voice coming from a distance. If she didn't get out, he would find her as she was—reduced to a pitiful, disgusting thing. The thought was unbearable. This place had changed her to someone she didn't even recognize, but one trait did remain—her pride. She would bury herself under a rubble of rocks before letting Sterling witness her dignity's collapse.

Diedre gathered the fragments of her strength; she called upon her instinct for survival. If she was to survive, she had no choice but to leave of her own volition and cling to an irrevocable vow: She might never recover from her emotional mauling, but she would *not* be broken.

Crawling out, Diedre glanced back. Just once. "My place," she said in a raw voice. "I'll miss you."

Spine straight and head high, she strode away from the man calling her name. The shore was her destination, but she had to say good-bye to the places where her memories ran too deep.

The lagoon's crystal water winked a remembrance—her first bath here, with Sterling guarding her from himself. Her period; his lust and compassion. The storm beating her down; Sterling carrying her to safety . . . and home. Her ears filling with a Tarzan yell before strong arms swept her up and they flew into the air on the wings of love and a vine.

She saw herself weeping over her first rabbit; Sterling making her kill it, then holding her while he said proudly that she had what it took. The rock tunnel filled her vision, the hallowed place where he'd stalked her, then flushed her out to stake his claim. *Their mating.* Her fear; his masterful induction into the rites of passion.

Diedre's throat closed; she struggled to take a breath. She blinked away stinging tears and turned her back.

Their cave. She saw it looming near and heard their conversation as he'd introduced her to their home.

Diedre looked down at the bodice he'd mended, the shorts. She touched the abalone comb in her hair. The memories they'd made in their cave were too poignant. She walked away, forcing her feet to move to the shore and waiting craft.

Sterling caught her arm just before she reached it. "Diedre, we have to talk. You *have* to listen to me."

His touch seared her skin; it seared her heart. It was more than she could stand. Her strength couldn't hold her together if she looked into his eyes. And so she looked away . . . and saw Ming.

Gathering the remnants of her wavering courage, she broke free without a word.

"I feel no pain," she whispered as she walked stoically to civilization. "I feel no pain."

The trip to Florida was made in a taut silence. Diedre felt her torment mingle with envy and confusion and bitterness.

She couldn't look at Sterling, especially when she could feel his eyes boring down on her. Pleading. Loving. Asking forgiveness and understanding. Why had he not told her before? She had no idea, but knowing him, she was sure he must have felt his reasons were justified.

"Diedre," Ming called over the whirr of blades

slicing air. "The tower just radioed. Your parents are already on their way. You are glad?"

Diedre glanced up. Ming's face was more than beautiful; it was serene, gentle, compassionate. She hated it. Her only answer to Ming was a hostile silence. Then, remembering her vow of pride, Diedre managed a curt nod.

"Diedre, I like your clothes. Maybe we can visit sometime. I . . . if we could be friends someday . . . you may let me try them on?"

Over my dead body. They're mine. He's mine.

And apparently Ming's too.

Diedre risked a furtive glance at Sterling. He was staring straight ahead, caught in his own private hell. She hoped he hurt. She hoped he hurt so bad, he wanted to throw himself overboard and break into a thousand tiny pieces. If he was that torn up, then maybe he was half as shattered for having betrayed her as she was by his betrayal. She knew he would never have deliberately destroyed her trust, but that fact did nothing to alter reality.

After Diedre refused her adversary's attempt at friendship, Ming granted her enough mercy to turn away and say no more. The remainder of the flight was interminable. The hours it took seemed like days, but then the chopper finally made its final descent.

"We've got a crowd," the pilot announced. "Looks like a welcoming party. Sorry, you two. Even from here I can see the press and cameras."

The helicopter landed, and almost immediately the passenger door was pulled open. She could already hear the fanfare, the sick curiosity hovering outside.

Ming got out. Sterling reached over and offered Diedre his hand. She ignored it. To touch him was to invite her own hysterical undoing in full sight of the onlookers waiting to get the exciting story.

What a story she could give them, she thought

derisively, a real-life Hollywood drama, with adventure, danger, passion, and love. Betrayal and violent emotion.

She shunned Sterling's gaze just as she'd disdained his hand, and made her way out alone. Lights flashed, microphones were held up while reporters bombarded her ears with questions. She cringed and commanded herself not to vault back to the helicopter's safety. Then she saw her parents rush forward.

Mother was crying. Father was calling her name. And Sterling was gripping her arm.

"I'll call you," he said in a tight, urgent voice.

"Save the quarter. I won't answer the phone." She knew she couldn't endure speaking to him again while Ming wore his ring. "Good-bye," she said, unable to say his name. "It's been . . . enlightening."

She couldn't look at him, and glanced away, only to collide with Ming's gaze. Caring. A quiet understanding.

Ming embraced her, and Diedre feared she might break and sob against the slight shoulder. How could Sterling not love a woman such as this? One who was tender, who felt sympathy for her rival? Never had she felt so small.

Diedre refrained from returning the embrace and stiffened.

"Thank you," she said. "And please, thank your grandfather. He must be an extraordinary man."

"He would like you. Very much. When we return, I will tell him of the woman warrior who lived with Sterling."

She couldn't bear it. Her parents were calling to her. Cameras clicked. And Sterling? He was taking her hands.

"These belong to you," he said quietly, tender emotion threading his words. "I *will* call. Please . . . answer."

Diedre felt her fingers close around the soft fur of a

rabbit's foot, the jagged edge of a fish comb. They nestled beside a sheathed Swiss Army knife, and there was no mistaking the bite of the star blade. Three she would take. One she could not.

She pressed the Grandmaster's star back into Sterling's palm. "I wish you both well. Be healthy, be happy, and give the Grandmaster my regrets that we never met."

She thrust herself away and waded past the voices and fanfare to her parents' open arms. They had an escort, and for once she was grateful for their clout. Climbing into the waiting limousine, she gave herself permission for one fleeting backward glance.

Sterling watched Diedre being embraced by her family, then disappearing into the security of a long, black limousine. When she turned around, he saluted her.

Even from a distance he could see her convulsive swallow, the way she fought the tears. He understood what had compelled her actions; how costly the price she'd paid. He bowed low, giving her his ultimate respect and honor.

The star bit into his clenched fist.

No, Diedre, you were wrong. This belongs to you. You've done what I never could, leaving with nothing but yourself and inner strength. You're much stronger, darlin', than your mate who wouldn't have made it half this far.

As Sterling watched the car streak away, he acknowledged a humbling truth.

Diedre possessed the ninja spirit he continually strived for, but lacked the capacity to find.

Sixteen

"Diedre, darling, we were so worried about you." Her mother reached for her hand and held it tight.

The limousine cut a sharp corner, and Sterling disappeared from view. Diedre forced her gaze away from the window, the image of his deep, symbolic bow etched into her memory to join too many others.

"We thought . . . we thought we'd lost our little girl." Her father's voice was choked.

Commanding herself to block out the jumbled emotions she couldn't yet deal with, she concentrated on her parents' outpour of concern and . . . love.

"That man you were with. He looked so dangerous." Her mother shivered. "Especially with that scar. Not to mention the way he was dressed."

"Mother, take a look at me."

"I have. Oh, Diedre, to think what you must have gone through . . . It's appalling. We'll stop and buy you new clothes before we take you back home."

Home? Where was home? On a faraway island she would never see again, just as she might never see Sterling again.

"Driver, stop at the nearest clothing store." Alexander Forsythe put his arm around his daughter's shoulder and hugged her. "We came right away, but we left instructions to have your room made ready for you."

"No."

"What?"

"You heard me, Mother and Father. I said, *no*." She leaned forward and tapped the chauffeur's shoulder. "Forget the store. What I've got on is fine."

"Really, Diedre, you can't be serious!"

"I most certainly am." Diedre stroked the beloved pelt riding her hips. She wasn't ready to give up the last traces of her primal persona. "I appreciate your concern, but I'm not going home with you either. If you want to help, you'll just get me back to Fond du Lac as soon as possible."

"But that's ridiculous. You've been through an ordeal. Come home with us. You can rest there." Her mother's gaze was pleading. "Besides, Madame Lestat said if you were ever found, she would take you back at the opera company. There's still a chance you could win a role, not a lead, of course, but—"

"I won't do that, Mother. I'm sorry, but opera's your love, not mine." Diedre looked from her mother to her father, both apparently taken aback by her assertiveness. "You have to realize I'm not the same person I used to be. I'm a grown woman, and it's time you accepted that fact. You have no choice but to let me lead my own life. Now please, take me to *my* home. I'll come visit you as soon as I work through some things I have to deal with alone and in my own way."

Her parents exchanged astonished glances, then turned their attention to Diedre with expressions revealing respect, an acknowledgment that she was their equal as an adult.

"Very well," her father said, then gave instructions to the driver to backtrack to their private plane.

Diedre was relieved when she saw the curiosity-seekers had disbanded, and Sterling was nowhere in sight. She craved even a glimpse of his face; but she knew it would only melt the fragile barrier of ice protecting her heart. Getting away was imperative. She didn't want to break down in front of her parents, especially now that she had established her independence once and for all.

The trip to Wisconsin was made amid careful, probing questions, which she deflected with monosyllabic answers. She made it back to her small apartment and successfully sent her parents away. The landlord's shock at seeing her was enough to coax a weary smile from her lips.

The older woman groped for words to explain that she hadn't known whom to contact and had felt peculiar about removing Diedre's things. The market was slow, and so no new renters had emerged to take her place.

Her place. Diedre supposed this was the closest she would get to her island getaway. A promise to pay the back rent assured her a new key.

Now she looked around her. Everything was as she'd left it. Books everywhere. Darjeeling tea and china cups on the counter. She would brew a cup, reacquaint herself with the amenities of civilized life, do anything to keep from facing the inevitable.

Utilities were included, so the water was still on. She turned the faucet and watched with something close to amazement as water gushed from the spigot. How odd it seemed, as odd as the sound of cars outside. It was the same sense of strangeness she'd felt peering from the limo's window and seeing the rush of traffic against the backdrop of buildings and the medley of people on the streets.

The bathroom was far from a lagoon. Bathtub. Toilet. Sink. All so civilized, so alien. The images blurred, and her throat constricted. She didn't belong here anymore. Just as the clothes she thumbed through in her closet were too prim, too restrictive. They had been owned by someone hiding beneath layers of fabric, behind the pages of a book. She tested the bed. The mattress was too giving, too soft. Diedre didn't like it. The hardwood floor was closer to the cave's floor, and the rug reminiscent of their pallet.

She lay down, her cheek cushioned by the cool wood. For a while she didn't cry; she simply lay there alone, too alone.

A low moaning sound came from somewhere. Perhaps from this woman grappling for her sanity while it rushed away on the sound of a wave hitting sand, then retreating to the sea, leaving her bereft of any comfort she could cling to.

Diedre stretched out, seeking mercy from God. Didn't He feel her heart shatter? Couldn't He see her open wound? Perhaps He heard her plea for release, for the first tear finally rolled down her cheek, and then another and another until her face was bathed and her head slid against a puddle of liquid.

She wept until she was dry, and then she wept dryly. Her sobs were bitter and wretched, and instinctively she reached for her mate. Where was Sterling? He should be holding her now, soothing her with words of comfort while he locked her tight in a lover's embrace.

Her fingers clenched, but she grasped nothing. The emptiness stretched into infinity, and she stared into a never-ending hell.

You're strong, darlin'. You're a survivor because you've got what it takes.

She heard his voice as clearly as if he stood there. It stoked a need in her to prove his words were true. Diedre picked herself up. She swallowed a sob and went to the bureau drawer where she'd placed her treasured keepsakes. She stroked her fingertips over the nicked Swiss Army knife. Then, taking the comb made of a polished fish spine, she worked it through her mane of bleached hair. The comb caught a tangle, and a hard tug broke off a piece of smooth bone.

Hands shaking, she carefully put the comb and the broken bone back with the knife. Diedre stared at herself in the mirror. What she saw was a face that bore the evidence of tears and emotional trauma. The same face reflected maturity and strength. Her fingers closed around the rabbit's foot.

Taking it with her to the kitchen, where a teakettle whistled, she stroked it across her still-wet cheek. Diedre knew her loss could not be endured. But because she was a survivor, she had no choice but to endure it.

A week later she still survived. Diedre entered the library, ready to assume the position she'd left. No problem, her supervisor had said; they couldn't wait to have her back. The person who'd been hired to take over her duties hadn't worked out. In fact, the position of head librarian was opening up, and would she be interested in applying?

After getting through the necessary ritual of greetings and too many personal questions asked, Diedre stared around her with little enthusiasm. How dry reading had been since her return. She'd read everything she could find on the Bermuda Triangle, but the vicarious thrill of reading about adventures was gone now that she'd lived through her own. The fictional adventures and romances she'd filled her time with had only made her hunger for more of the real thing.

The day passed slowly. Diedre went home, exhausted from work's demands and fending off her curious coworkers, as well as the plague of memories she struggled to keep at bay. She checked her phone, which had been reconnected the day before. The answering machine blinked, indicating messages.

"Diedre, it's Mother. Thank goodness your phone's working again. We've been calling every day. We . . . well, we know you can take care of yourself, but we're worried about you. Please, dear, call us tonight. If you can break away this weekend, we'd love to have you come visit so we can talk. It's important to us. We—" There was a pause. "We do love you. You know that, don't you?"

The click sounded, and Diedre made a mental note to call back before she went to bed. She could handle her parents now, and a visit would be nice. They might never be as close as some families, but there was no reason for estrangement.

"Diedre." The second message began to play, and she felt a jolt, a sensation akin to an elbow in her stomach, while her legs quivered and almost buckled.

"I'm calling from Japan. I don't know when I can get back, but we have to talk. This is where I can be reached." Sterling recited the overseas number. "Before you cut me off, listen to me. The Grandmaster's very ill, and I'm having to deal with a lot of things I can't go into right now. I'm sure you must resent me. Hell, I hate myself for what I've put you through. Just remember one thing—I love you. I—"

Diedre tore the tape from the machine, mangling it with icy fingers attached to sweating palms. She was trembling from head to foot, and she crumpled to the floor. The sound of his voice had been too incisive, stripping away her tentative control.

He loved her. She knew that; not for a moment had she doubted it. Yet he had loved another long before her, a woman he'd loved enough to ask her to marry him.

The questions never quit coming; they assaulted her even in sleep. How long had he courted Ming?

What presents had he given her over the years? She couldn't bear to think of him kissing her, making love to her—as surely he had by now. It was only natural, wasn't it? Even if Sterling initially resisted, how long could he deny his lovely wife-to-be her intimate rights? A vision of his strong dark hands moving over Ming's delicate porcelain body made her moan and bite her fist until she tasted blood.

Would they mate gently, unlike the rapacious couplings that had defined her and Sterling's own emotional bonding in a world that no longer existed? Her soul was eternally his, but Sterling was now straddled between loyalties and love for two women.

Diedre looked at the mangled tape she'd flung to the floor. She had to protect herself. If hearing his message could leave her so emotionally unstrung, she knew there was no possibility she could get through an actual conversation without coming apart at the seams.

She unplugged the phone. It would stay that way unless she needed to make a call. As a survivor, she could not put herself in jeopardy by giving him access to her ears and heart. She needed time and distance to strengthen the weak link holding her together.

Two weeks passed. As Diedre trudged home after another dull workday, she smiled, remembering the recent visit with her parents. At least some things worked out. She shuffled through the day's assortment of mail, while she kicked the door shut with her high-heeled pump.

Bills fluttered to the floor along with Ed McMahon announcing her million-dollar chance. Then her hands began to sweat. Her body shook. She didn't need the Japanese stamps or postmark to identify the handwriting she'd never seen before.

His script was bold and large, like the man himself.

Just looking at it made her long anew for the time they didn't have the luxury pen or paper. She kissed the envelope. She began to weep.

What was inside? An apology? The assurance of his love . . . along with his regrets that he'd come to a heartrending decision? If so, she knew he wouldn't be so cruel as to include a wedding invitation.

Diedre pressed the unopened letter to her breast. The possibilities were many, and she craved to read his words. But the wound broke open as fresh as the day she'd said good-bye. *Not yet*, her instinct for self-preservation whispered. *Not yet*.

She would open the letter—when she was strong enough to withstand whatever Sterling might have to say.

"Books on survival? Certainly, right this way."

Diedre led yet another library patron to the requested section. *You want to know about survival?* she felt like saying. *You're talking to a pro. How about four unopened, tear-streaked letters under my pillow at home?*

It had been six weeks since she first returned, and she realized if she wasn't strong enough by now, she never would be. Making her way back to her desk near the front, she came to a decision. She would buy a bottle of sake if she could find one after work, and open the letters one by one.

Her head was bent over a stack of requests for topics from A to Z when she sensed someone standing in front of her desk. Odd, she hadn't heard any footsteps or even a whisper of breath.

"I'm looking for books on the Bermuda Triangle. Maybe you could suggest a few?"

Diedre's head snapped up. Her gaze collided with intense, kaleidoscopic eyes that were boring into hers. The face was beloved, too familiar. A scar marked his cheek, and a cleft dipped into the jut of his shaven chin.

Sterling parked a hip against her desk and leaned down. The loincloth had been traded for a crisp white shirt and tailored khaki pants.

Her heart began to beat too fast, or perhaps it wasn't beating at all. She couldn't speak. She couldn't blink. Why was he here? And why didn't he say something while she gaped at him as though he were a too-good-to-be-true mirage?

Diedre pushed away from the desk, or at least she thought she did. Her wobbly legs began to move, but she was too numb to feel them.

"Follow me," she said in a shaking voice. Her gaze darted from the tilted angle of books to the tight, pursed lips belonging to the man who kept pace beside her and continued to stare at her with a mixture of tenderness and purpose.

Questions crowded in her mind, making her so confused, she forgot which direction she was going. Was he here out of guilt? Did his sense of honor demand that he put things right with his island comrade?

Each silent step of the way heightened her anxiety until she thought she might scream from the consuming need to touch him, to feast her gaze on his face. On automatic pilot, Diedre led them to a deserted aisle. The tension between them and inside her was unbearable. She couldn't see the titles or authors, but she reached for a familiar book.

Sterling abruptly caught her wrist. She stared at his fingers and felt the scalding heat of his touch. Slowly, she slid her gaze up his arm and massive chest. The cleft in his chin begged her to fit her tongue into the dimple. His lips were unsmiling. His eyes were narrowed, and his laser-sharp gaze speared her to the quick.

"You didn't return my call."

"I . . . I couldn't."

"You didn't answer my letters."

His fingertips seared the nerve endings of her skin. He pulled her closer and she turned in, like steel drawn to a magnet. His eyes—hurt, angry, demanding an answer—were searching hers.

"I didn't read them," she confessed, suddenly feeling that her need for self-protection had been the coward's way out.

"Why not?" His breath was close to her ear and raised the fine hair on the back of her neck.

"It was necessary, Sterling. I didn't know any other way to survive."

"We survive together, Diedre."

"But Ming—"

"Is in love with someone else, just as I am. You'd already know that if you had bothered to call or read one of my letters."

Her mind was spinning, and her heart was racing. Heaven opened up, and she flew on a wing. He was back. He had come back *for her!* She was trembling from the inside out. She wanted to hear his voice, his rough reassurance again, again, again. . . .

"You . . . you mean, you're not marrying Ming? But the Grandmaster—"

"Is much better. As soon as he started to recuperate, we had a long talk. He wished Ming and me only happiness, if not together, then in the separate paths we're compelled to take."

He grasped her shoulders and gave her a single, fierce shake. "You ran," he said between tight lips. "You put me through hell, and I'm back with a savage's thirst for revenge."

"Take your revenge." She clenched him to her in a fevered embrace. "I'll never run again."

"Damn right you won't." He backed her against the stack of books, his purpose as apparent as the time he'd stalked her to stake his claim. "A woman does not run from her mate."

Sterling's hand met the pins restraining her hair. His low growl echoed between her ears at the same time that she felt his impatient fingers doing away with the pins. He thrust them aside and tangled his hand into the long, bleached strands. He pulled her head back and pressed his mouth against her neck.

"You are my mate," he said roughly. "Say it."

"I am your mate," she vowed.

Her pulse leaped, the blood surging wildly through her veins and throbbing against his tongue, the nip of his teeth. He grazed her jaw and sucked her chin before his lips slanted over hers and they met in a deep, soulful kiss.

It was the kiss of lovers deprived too long, a melding of souls claiming the same destiny. Their hunger escalated to a mutual ravishment.

"Oh, excuse me!" someone gasped.

Before Diedre could recover, Sterling broke the torrid kiss and hoisted her over his shoulder. With long, powerful strides he plowed a decisive track down the aisle and through the main library.

"Sterling! What do you think you're doing?" she whispered sharply, unable to miss the shocked expressions of the gawking onlookers. "I work here!"

He swatted her squirming rear end and said firmly, "Not for long, you don't." He stopped for a split second at the front desk. "Tell them, Diedre."

Hanging over his shoulder, Diedre looked sideways into the startled face of a coworker.

"I—I'm taking the day off." Sterling bumped her against his shoulder in warning. "Actually, I'm not sure when I'll be back. Something's come up"—she heard his seductive chuckle—"and . . . well, I may be vanishing again."

With a quick about-face he marched out like a pirate with his stolen booty, and they emerged into

the brisk October air peppered with drifting snow-
flakes. Sterling tossed her into the backseat of a
limousine and landed on top of her.

"Let's cruise, James. You've got the address. Hit the
gas."

"You've got it, Mr. Jakes. We're on our way!" The
driver peeled out of the library parking lot the moment Sterling slammed the tinted privacy window
shut.

"Okay, woman, now it's just you and me and thirty
miles of uninterrupted asphalt."

Diedre laughed, the first real laugh she'd had in
nearly two months. "Are we headed to the Casbah?"

"Nothing that civilized. But in the meantime, darlin', let's try something we haven't done before. It's
called making out in the backseat of a car."

He didn't give her time to argue, and Diedre decided it was just as well. She was perfectly ecstatic to
return the provocative thrusts of his tongue, the
bites on the neck, the grinding of hips between
murmurs of love.

By the time they arrived, she was in a dire state of
want. Judging from the way Sterling hauled her out
and carried her over his shoulder with all the finesse
of a caveman, so was he.

"A motel!" Diedre glanced from the upside-down
room number to her mate's backside.

"Not on your life, darlin'. I brought you where we
used to live. Or at least as close as we can get."

The door yawned open at the same time he jostled
her into his arms.

The jagged molded plaster on the doorway resembled the mouth of their cave. He ducked inside and
carried her past a deep, roiling spa with tortoiseshell
tile. Silk ficus and palms created the illusion of a
lagoon deep in a jungle terrain.

"Where *are* we?" The last word ended on a gasp as
Sterling tossed her onto a big, round water bed and

loomed tall against the backdrop of a stone ceiling. Primitive, sensual music pulsed around them, filling her ears and storming her veins.

"Most people know it as the LeCave at West Bend's Best Western FantaSuites. But we're not most people, so we'll just pretend it's home."

"Then we should christen it, and the sooner, the better." Diedre stretched out on the bed and eagerly reached for him. Lovemaking was the intimate remedy that would soothe the hurt of their rapidly mending hearts and seal the destiny of their souls.

"Not yet, darlin'. You wait here and get ready to make up for lost time. Before we consummate the bargain, I've got that bottle of sake I promised you a long time ago. It's waiting by the lagoon."

Diedre crossed her arms over her chest and embraced the two women inside her. Not for love or money would she let this man out of her civilized arms or primitive clutches again.

She was staring at the simulated rock ceiling when Sterling approached on silent feet. Without warning he pounced and landed on all fours above her.

They wrestled and grappled and laughed and kissed until Sterling lay on top. All play suddenly ceased. He kissed the ring finger on her left hand and held her eyes with a solemn gaze.

"Marry me," he softly commanded. "I've got two tickets to Japan for next week. The Grandmaster's expecting to meet my wife while we're on our honeymoon."

Diedre stroked the scar on his cheek while she stared into his searching eyes. Then, with a ninjutsu technique, she switched their places in a blink. Gazes locked, naked, hot, teeming with love and devotion.

"Grrrr," she growled. She sealed her vow with a savage kiss.

In the following scene, Amy has been daydreaming while working in the vineyards, when she is distracted by her fellow grape-pickers grumbling about another worker. Fascinated by the descriptions, Amy looked up . . .

In the years that followed she would always remember that moment. She would relive it as if watching a movie inside her mind, the colors and sounds extraordinarily vivid, the dramatic impact staggering. He stood perhaps a hundred feet from them, outlined by a nearly tangible solitude, very still, studying a cluster of grapes crushed in one big fist. He was tall, with an elegant kind of brawniness to his body. Amy stared. His mystery excited her imagination.

Grape juice ran down his arm. There was weary anger in the set of his shoulders, and remnants of violence in the way he clenched the pulpy mass of burst fruit. Juice dripped onto his bare feet. His white T-shirt was stained with sweat down the center and under the arms; his baggy, wrinkled pants were an ugly green color soiled with red clay at the knees. They hung low on his hips as if about to fall off. Only a loosely knotted tie-string kept them from slipping.

He wore no hat, and his thick, charcoal-black hair was disheveled. Dark beard stubble shadowed his cheeks. His eyes were covered by unremarkable black sunglasses, but his face, making a strong, blatantly masculine profile, was anything but unremarkable.

He slung the grapes to the ground, staggering a little as he did. Then, wielding a pair of razor-sharp clippers so swiftly that Amy gasped with fear, he snipped a small cluster of grapes and shoved it into his mouth. He stripped it with one ferocious tug of his teeth then slung the empty stem over his shoulder.

"A cocky drunk, ain't he?" someone muttered.

Amy gaped at him. The others chuckled. At any second Beaucaire would come thundering down the aisle of trellises and raise hell. It would be spectacular entertainment.

What would the newcomer do next? For a man who was dirty and apparently soused, he had an aura of graceful arrogance. But then he went to a trellis post and leaned there heavily, resting his head on one arm. He no longer looked imposing. Fatigue seemed to drag at every muscle of his body. Amy clenched her hands, feeling a misfit's sympathy for another misfit but wanting to scold him for making a fool of himself.

She didn't dare. He looked dangerous—his hands were big-knuckled and dirty; ropy muscles flexed in his forearms. He wore his solitude like a shield. He swayed and stared fixedly at the ground, as if searching for a place to fall. But after a moment he dropped his clippers into a bucket and shoved himself away from the post. Staggering, he headed for a wooden crate that sat at the far end of a row. When he arrived there he disappeared around the corner.

Amy waited breathlessly for him to reappear. He didn't.

"Go get Mr. Beaucaire," someone said.

She swung toward the others. "No! I'll go see what he's doing. Don't say anything to Mr. Beaucaire. I mean it!"

Everyone stared at her. It was the first time they'd heard her speak in full sentences. She was shocked by the outburst, herself. "I, uhmmm, I b-bet he's just sick."

"Well, Lord have mercy. We finally heard Olive Oyl make more than a squeak."

Everyone chortled. Amy was mortified. Her voice humiliated her when she forgot to restrain it. People laughed at her behind her back; all through school her classmates had made fun of her. She clamped her lips together and ground her teeth as if she could crush whatever it was that made her sound the way she did. She dreaded getting a job where she had to talk. She stayed awake at night worrying about it.

But now she shoved embarrassment aside and hurried toward the crate, her heart in her throat. Behind her a woman called, "You leave that feller alone! We're gonna go get Mr. Beaucaire!"

Amy kept walking. Maybe she sympathized with all the ne'er-do-wells of the world, or maybe she was an expert on mean drunks. But she felt that there was some good reason for this man's problem.

Uncertainty pooled in her stomach. Slowing down, she crept up to the crate and stopped to listen. She heard only the rustle of grape leaves as the hot wind stroked the vineyard. Tiptoeing in the brittle grass, she sidled up to the crate's back corner and peeked around.

He lay on his back. He had removed the T-shirt and stuffed it under his head as a pillow. His hairy chest held her attention as it rose and fell in slow rhythm. His hands lay beside his head, palms up, dirty and stained with grape juice but graceful-looking nonetheless.

She stepped forward in silent awe. He slept, but there was nothing vulnerable or relaxed about his face. His mouth remained shut and firm. Above the black sunglasses a frown pulled at his brows. Up close he looked younger than she'd expected, perhaps no more than thirty.

She shifted from one foot to the other, gazing at his sleeping form in consternation. Maybe it would be best just to leave him to his fate. She bent over and sniffed. The scent of his sweat mingled with the sweet aroma of grapes, red clay, and a faint antiseptic smell that puzzled her. She knew the smell of booze and pot; neither was present.

Reassured, she knelt beside him. She removed her sunglasses and tucked them in her shirt pocket. Her hand trembling, she reached out and touched his shoulder. "Hey. Hey, wake up."

A jolt of awareness ran through him. He lifted his head and froze. She jerked her hand back. His eyes were hidden behind the glasses, but she felt as if he were scrutinizing her angrily. She fumbled with the water bottle on her belt. There was nothing else to do except blunder onward and hope he didn't yell at her.

"You gotta get up," she urged, holding the bottle toward him. "You'll get fired if you stay here. Come on, have a drink of water. You'll be okay. Get up."

When he neither moved nor replied, her nervousness gave way to exasperation. "Don't be a j-jerk! You look like you need this job! Now take a drink of water! Uhmmm, *Habla usted ingles? Si?* No? Come on, that's all the Spanish I know! Say something!"

"I would rather listen to you say something. You say quite enough for both of us, and I like your voice."

She stared at him, mesmerized. His English was excellent, but accented. The accent was not Spanish, though she couldn't identify it. His voice sank into her senses—rich, deep, beautiful. Fatigue made it hoarse, but the effect was unforgettable.

"Here," she squeaked, thrusting the water bottle close to his mouth. "This'll make you feel better."

He let his head rest on the wadded shirt again. Exhaustion creased the sides of his mouth. "Thank you, but no." He raised a hand and pushed the bottle away. "I need only to rest."

She didn't know why, but she was desperate to keep him out of trouble. He must be too tired and sick to think straight. "You're gonna get fired!"

"No, I assure you—"

"Take a sip." Amy stuck the long plastic tube between his lips and squeezed the bottle hard. He tried to swallow the jet of water and nearly strangled. Shoving the bottle away, he sat up and began coughing.

A stream of melodic non-English purled from his throat, and she didn't have to understand it to know that he was disgusted. She clutched the water bottle to her chest.

As he finished he whipped his glasses off and turned a stern gaze on her. Dread filled her chest, but she was too stunned to do anything except stare back. No one would call him pretty; in fact, his nose was blunt and crooked, his cheekbones jagged, and his mouth almost too masculine. It was a tough Bogart mouth, and the effect was heightened by a thin white scar that started an inch below his bottom lip and disappeared under his chin.

But all that made him handsome in a way she'd never encountered before. And his eyes, large and darkly lashed in the tough face, seemed to have been inherited from a different, more elegant heritage.

"Are you . . . you're not one of the regular workers," she said in confusion.

"No."

"Are you sick or something?"

"Or something." His expression was pensive for a moment. "I am only tried . . . just tired . . . It will pass."

"Oh. Okay. Sorry to pester you." She started to rise. He clasped her arm.

"Don't leave. I didn't mean to chase you away. Here. Give me the water. Perhaps you're right. It helps."

While she watched in amazement he drank slowly from the bottle. She spent an awkward moment gazing at the silky movement of muscles in his neck and chest. He lowered the bottle and studied her some more. The skin around his lips was tight and pale. He blinked in groggy thought, then handed the bottle back. "You make me feel remarkably better. *Merci*." His mouth curved in a private, off-center smile that erased all sternness from his face.

Amy caught her breath. Her shyness returned like a smothering blanket. *Merci*. He was *French*. Maurice Chevalier. The Eiffel Tower. Paris. Tongue kissing. "Don't pass out, okay? Bye."

CIRCLE OF PEARLS
by Rosalind Laker

When Julia Palliser was born one October day in 1641, a rare and beautiful Elizabeth drop-pearl was placed in her tiny palm. It symbolized the only remaining gown of Elizabeth I's extensive wardrobe—a pearl-encrusted gift from Julia's grandmother, a legacy binding three generations of women.

All her life she has loved Christopher Wren, the brilliant mathematican and architect who would one day help to rebuild London. Why then is she irresistibly drawn to Adam Warrender, the enemy her stepfather wants her to marry?

In the following scene, Julia weds the man she never dreamed of loving . . .

Certain moments stood out in her mind afterwards. The gold ring sliding onto her finger. The surprising tenderness of Adam's kiss in the vestry before they signed the register there and the fragrance of her Sotherleigh posy when Mary, who had held it for her during the service, handed it back to her. Then walking down the aisle with her fingers on Adam's wrist while everyone smiled and nodded and the organ made the air tremble. Among the sea of faces only Christopher's stood out, but she did not allow herself to meet his eyes. This was Adam's day and in the compromise she had arranged with herself she could not fail him in what was rightfully his. Her golden shoes bore her on her way out into the sunshine with the man she had married.

It was a light-hearted ride home and from the village onwards there were petals in the path of the coach. Near the gates she and Adam threw showers of silver coins and were cheered and applauded right to the door of Sotherleigh.

Sotherleigh had not seen such feasting and merriment for many years. Wine flowed and dish after dish was borne in to replenish the long table in the Great Hall and the extra tables that had been added. Speeches were made and toasts drunk while musicians played in the gallery, sometimes barely to be heard above the chatter and the laughter. In a meadow that lay the same distance from both Sotherleigh and Warrender half an ox was being roasted, and mutton turned on spits as the tenants of both estates celebrated the marriage, barrels set up to supply them with all the ale they could drink.

Adam and Julia led their guests into the dancing in an adjoining room. When Michael partnered her they exchanged a glance as the measure took them past the Queen's Door.

"If only I had known," she said on a sigh, referring obliquely to their talk at breakfast.

"Hush," he replied with a slight shake of his head. "Think no more about it. This is a time for rejoicing, not for regrets."

She was not entirely sure about that, but then he did not know of the emotional turmoil she had been through and which was not yet over. Fortunately it was proving easy to enjoy herself. Even with Christopher as she whirled in a country dance, her merriment was spontaneous and her laughter full of delight. He had heard that he was to be appointed the Savilian professor of Astronomy at Oxford, the most tremendous honor to be bestowed on a man as young as he.

"You're turning upside down the custom of having greybeards in high places," she declared teasingly.

"It will be a few months before I take up the appointment and maybe I'll have turned grey myself by then," he joked, holding her hand high as she danced under his arm.

"You'll always be young, even when you're old in years," she insisted, half seriously and half in jest.

"How can you be sure of that?" he asked in the same vein.

"In this gown and my golden slippers I can be sure of anything today." Playfully she kissed the tip of her finger and placed it against his mouth. Then the shifting pattern of the dance swept her away as another partner claimed her and he continued the measure with Anne, who skipped light as a feather.

Time, speeding by, brought the supper hour when every guest found the traditional gift by the places set at the tables. There were elaborately cuffed and scented gauntlets for the men and white kid gloves perfumed with a floral fragrance for the women. Again the feasting was prolonged, noisy singing increasing among those getting drunker than the rest.

Julia, chatting to those sitting opposite her at the head table, failed to notice when the singers were hushed and an amused and expectant silence began to fall on the jovial company. Every head was turned in her direction. With a start she saw that Susan and Mary and Faith had come to her chair. It was time for her to be escorted upstairs by her ladies. A blush flared into her face and then she recovered herself. As she rose from her chair Adam, sitting beside her, was the first on his feet and the whole assembly followed suit. With dignity she acknowledged the cheers and raised glasses as she began to proceed from the Great Hall.

In the bedchamber of the apartment that had been Katherine's, Julia was suddenly assailed by a rush of panic as Mary began to unlace the back of her gown. Sarah, assisted by Molly, had spread the linen sheet on which Julia stood to prevent the Elizabethan gown from coming in contact with the floor when it fell about her feet. But she was reluctant to disrobe. She had not minded when Susan had removed the coronet of roses, faded now, from her head or when the pearl ear-bobs and the necklet had been replaced in the silver casket held by Faith, but the gown was another matter. It had sustained her throughout the day, given her a light heart when otherwise her earlier melancholy could have stayed unrelentingly with her.

She crossed her arms and held the gown by the sleeves as the released lacing at the back caused it to slip down from her shoulders. She wondered what these five women in the room would say if she said she would not care how she was ravished in the night if she could keep this gown on her body.

"Step out of your gown now," Susan said quite firmly, seeing that she delayed. "It will not be long before Adam is escorted here."

Julia obeyed and felt the gown slip from her like a farewell caress, leaving her vulnerable and armorless. Sarah picked it up while Molly gathered up the discarded petticoats and stockings, removing them with the sheet after they had both bobbed to the bride and wished her a good night. Faith helped Julia into her nightgown.

"What a pretty garment this is!" Faith, modest to the extreme, thought such a soft cambric would be too revealing for her own choice, for the lace frill at the scooped neckline fell so low it almost revealed Julia's nipples, which could be clearly discerned. "Did you sew it yourself?"

"No, Mary did," Julia answered absently, sitting down before the mirror at her toilet table. "I've been too busy dealing in ribbons."

Faith was amazed. How could any girl be too busy to sew her own bridal nightgown? She had not realised quite how seriously Julia was taking her ribbon business.

Mary had finished brushing Julia's hair from its coiffure into the curls that danced down her back. Then it was Susan who saw her into bed and brought the sheet up over her breasts for concealment as she sat up against her pillows. From the distance there came a rising tumult of drunken voices raised in lewd songs and bursts of cheering.

"The bridegroom is on his way," Susan announced, glancing about the room to make sure that all was in order. The approaching din grew louder.

"Don't let all those people in!" Julia appealed urgently.

Susan nodded and guided Faith and Mary out into the parlour beyond where they formed a phalanx in front of the bedchamber door. It was to no avail. As the crowd of young men swarmed through into the apartment, all the older ones and the ladies remaining downstairs, the first to reach the three women simply picked them up with battle yells and, ignoring their protests, carried them forward into the bedchamber where they were set down on their feet again.

She looked for Adam and could not see him. Then there came a ripple through the gathering as those who had not yet managed to get into the bedchamber helped Michael and the groomsman push Adam through the jam in the doorway. For a few minutes he was wedged with the rest and then he was seized to be shoved and jostled towards the bed, people well-meaning but rough in their eagerness. He reached the foot in a dishevelled state with his dressing-robe torn and his nightshirt ripped from one shoulder. Leaning a hand against the carved bedpost, his grin was resigned as he recovered his breath.

Turning to Julia, Adam cupped the back of her head in his

hand and she tipped helplessly against him as he kissed her long and hard. The raucous approbation might have brought down a ceiling less well constructed than that of the Sotherleigh bedchamber. Still holding her head when the kiss ended, he put his cheek against hers and whispered in her ear. "That is what they wanted to see. Now they will go."

He was right. At last Susan was able to be in command again with Michael to assist her, although even then it took time before they were able to shepherd the last merry-maker out of the apartment back to the celebrations downstairs.

"Mary! Wait a moment!"

As Mary paused, surprised, Julia sprang from the bed to take up her bridal posy, which had been placed in a vase of water on a table. Careless of the drops spattering her nightgown, she rushed with it to Mary and put it into her hands.

"May you know joy in time to come!"

Mary's eyes filled with tears. Too choked to speak, she hugged Julia in gratitude and hurried away, forgetting to close the door. Slowly Julia pushed it shut. Then she stiffened. Without turning she knew that Adam had left the bed and was coming soundlessly towards her on his bare feet.

"That posy was well given, Julia."

Still she did not turn. "She is in love with my brother."

"I know."

"How?"

"She talks about him with shining eyes at the least excuse."

"Such is the weakness of lovers."

"Not with all, or else I should have shouted my love of you from the pinnacles of Westminster." He drew aside the curtain of her hair to place a kiss on the nape of her neck. Moving his hand down to her waist, he gently swivelled her round to face him and then kissed her, loving her mouth. To his joy her arms slid by her volition round his neck and he held her close, a new harmony created between them by the natural hunger of their young and healthy bodies, the fierce magnetism that had long been between them and his love that sought to find an answering chord in her.

When their kiss ended she laid her head against his shoulder. "I'm sure our marriage mended many feuds today."

He stroked one hand down her back. "There were new beginnings for quite a few people and especially for us."

"I think ours began when I put on my Elizabethan gown this morning. All day I saw it as the safeguard of happiness, a talisman without which everything would fade away again. It made me reluctant to discard it when my ladies brought me up here, but I need not have feared. What it ignited is still with me."

"Maybe it's because I have taken over its charge to be the protector of that happiness."

She raised her head and they looked deep into each other's eyes. "I want more than anything that we should fulfil each other's lives, no matter what is against us," she said quietly.

"There is nothing that we can't defeat together."

He kissed her again and she clung to him, hoping his words would prove true, for if their marriage failed to reach the heights the fault would be hers, of that she was sure. She wanted an end to being torn apart and for the compromise she had made to be a bridge to this man, although if it would take years or a lifetime she could not estimate. Love could not be driven out, but had to take its own time. Not even a new love had the power to banish the old completely if a wilful heart stood its ground.

"Take me to bed," she whispered. . . .

FOREVER
by Theresa Weir

New Fanfare author Theresa Weir will touch your hearts with FOREVER, a beautiful and passionate love story between two people who learn to live—and love—again. When journalist Sammy Thoreau loses much of his memory in a devastating car accident, doctors pronounce him a lost cause until Dr. Rachel Collins bravely takes on his case. But she doesn't expect Sammy, with his glittering dark eyes and sexy smile, to reverse their roles with a vengeance, to expose the secret pain she tries to hide, and to ignite forbidden emotions. . . .

In the following excerpt, Rachel lays eyes on her newest patient for the first time.

The majority of Rachel's cases were outpatients. A few were

sometimes hospitalized for short stays, but it had been over three years since she'd taken on anyone who might require long-term, intensive therapy, the kind that could be so emotionally draining. She hoped she was ready for it.

When she reached Samuel Thoreau's room, Rachel's first reaction was of indignation.

He was lying on his back on the bed. Even though he appeared to be totally sedated, his wrists were secured to the side rails, and he was wearing a green hospital gown with the word *Psycho* stenciled across the front in three-inch black letters.

"He arrived like this," the floor nurse whispered. "I got his blood pressure, but when I tried to take his temperature his teeth clamped down so hard on the thermometer I was afraid it might break off in his mouth. I wasn't sure what to do with him. . . ."

"We'll begin without restraints—harmless until proven otherwise."

"But Dr. Fontana said—"

"Mr. Thoreau is my patient, not Dr. Fontana's."

She approached the bed. The man's scalp was covered with a new crop of hair that was as inky black as his eyebrows. His face was hollow-cheeked and yellow-tinged—jaundiced, most likely from overmedication. He needed a shave and a bath and clean hospital clothes.

"Mr. Thoreau," she said softly, "I am Dr. Collins."

In a head injury case, the patient could appear to be totally incoherent when in actuality he wasn't. Rachel was always careful to guard her words, to not say anything that might cause undue distress.

"You're here at the University Hospital in La Grange, Iowa, because you were in an accident and hurt your head. I'm going to be helping to take care of you."

She watched his gaunt face for any sign of response and was rewarded with a slight movement beneath his closed lids.

"First of all, I'm going to make you more comfortable by untying your hands." She untied one, then the other. His arms fell limply to the bed.

She felt the pulse on his wrist. It was slow due to the overload of drugs in his system. Then she examined the area at the base of his skull, finding a small red ridge of scar tissue. No sign of infection. A miracle. He'd healed despite everything.

Rachel was about to call the nurse aside with further instructions when the man's eyelids twitched, then opened.

She found herself being regarded by a pair of coal-black eyes set deeply in bruised sockets. The look in them made her want to cry. Empty. Expecting nothing. Wanting nothing.

Once again, anger burned in her. How could anyone treat a patient this way? They had violated one of the important rules of medicine: First, do no harm. Apparently some institutions were still the stuff bad dreams were made of.

And then Samuel Thoreau did something that made her go weak with self-doubt, made her wonder if she'd just been fooling herself, made her fear that she might no longer have the emotional strength needed to survive this kind of journey, a journey that could take her deep into his psyche.

With defeated eyes, Samuel Thoreau looked up at her and whispered through dry lips, "I'll . . . be . . . good."

Several weeks later

It was Sunday morning. Rachel didn't usually stop at the hospital on Sundays, but she wanted to check on Sammy. He had been moved to a long-term facility, which meant he was in a larger room that was more like living quarters.

It was there that Rachel found him pacing back and forth.

As soon as her footfall sounded in the doorway, he swung around. The second he realized who it was, his frown turned to a smile. "Dr. Collins!" He bounded across the room, his energy buffeting her like a gust of ocean wind.

"I have a great idea. Let's go somewhere. Blow this hole for a while. What do you say?"

Restless, pent-up energy met bewildered sorrow. It took Rachel a moment to gather her thoughts.

"I could leave here for a while, couldn't I? Just an hour or two?"

The irrational side of her wanted to say yes. But the practical doctor knew he was too unpredictable, his psyche still too raw.

"Sammy . . . you're not quite ready. Maybe next week . . ."

"Next week!" He raked his fingers across his scalp, making his bristly hair stand on end. "I've got to get out of here," Sammy said, his voice edged with panic. "Just for a while. For an hour. A few minutes. I need to breathe."

His gaze shifted around the room, seeking a solution, seeking an escape, finally coming to light on her once more. "I'll be good, I swear." He drew a finger across his chest. "Cross my heart."

The desperation in his eyes was almost her undoing. What he was suggesting wasn't all that irregular. It was only a matter of signing a pass. But he wasn't ready. *She* wasn't ready.

He was watching her closely, the way he always did.

"You're not going to let me go, are you?" he asked.

"Sammy—"

"Don't say it. You don't have to say it. I can tell by your face."

He was moving toward her, closing the space between them. She took one step back, then another, until she was pressed to the wall with nowhere to run. And he was still coming.

"You're afraid," he stated. "What are you afraid of, Rachel?"

"Nothing."

"Tell me the truth. You're afraid of me, aren't you?"

"No."

"Yes. I've seen it in your face before, I can see it in your face now. Sometimes you look up from that clipboard of yours and catch me staring. And I can tell it bothers you. Why does it bother you, Rachel?" When she didn't answer, he asked, "Do you ever wonder what I'm thinking when I'm watching you?"

She swallowed.

"Want to know?"

She shook her head.

"No? But you're a shrink. You're supposed to want to hear my deepest, darkest secrets. Isn't that right? My deepest, darkest desires."

His voice was rough, threatening . . . and, heaven help her, sensual.

She brought up her hand. Fingers splayed, she pressed against his chest, trying to hold him back . . . but he didn't move. She knew she could scream for help and someone would come. But she also knew Sammy would never hurt her. At least not physically. But his words . . . they were a different thing altogether.

"Sometimes when I look at you," Sammy whispered, his face only inches from her, "I get horny. Did you know that, *Doctor* Collins?"

"Sammy." Once again she shoved the solidness of his chest, but it was like shoving something set in concrete.

"You know what else?" he asked slowly, thoughtfully. "A lot of times I wonder what it would be like to . . . *kiss* you."

From his emphasis on the word *kiss*, she knew he was insinuating much more than a kiss.

She felt her own panic wind higher. This had to stop. Immediately. "I'm your doctor. You're my patient. There can be nothing sexual between us."

"So *you* say."

"So the physician's rules of ethics say."

"Screw the rules. Screw ethics." His voice dropped, became more intimate. "Tell me, Rachel. How long's it been since you were . . . *kissed*?"

That inflection again. And now he pressed his body firmly against hers so they were touching from chest to knee.

His head came down, his mouth drawing nearer. . . .

THE EDITOR'S CORNER

With the six marvelous **LOVESWEPT**s coming your way next month, it certainly will be the season to be jolly. Reading the best romances from the finest authors—what better way to enter into the holiday spirit?

Leading our fabulous lineup is the ever-popular Fayrene Preston with **SATAN'S ANGEL**, LOVESWEPT #510. Nicholas Santini awakes after a car crash and thinks he's died and gone to heaven—why else would a beautiful angel be at his side? But Angel Smith is a flesh-and-blood woman who makes him burn with a desire that lets him know he's very much alive. Angel's determined to work a miracle on this magnificent man, to drive away the pain—and the peril—that torments him. A truly wonderful story, written with sizzling sensuality and poignant emotions—one of Fayrene's best!

How appropriate that Gail Douglas's newest LOVESWEPT is titled **AFTER HOURS**, #511, for that's when things heat up between Casey McIntyre and Alex McLean. Alex puts his business—and heart—on the line when he works *very* closely with Casey to save his newspaper. He's been betrayed before, but Casey inspires trust . . . and brings him to a fever pitch of sensual excitement. She never takes orders from anyone, yet she can't seem to deny Alex's passionate demands. A terrific book, from start to finish.

Sandra Chastain weaves her magical touch in **THE-JUDGE AND THE GYPSY**, LOVESWEPT #512. When Judge Rasch Webber unknowingly shatters her father's dream, Savannah Ramey vows a Gypsy's revenge: She would tantalize him beyond reason, awakening longings he's denied, then steal what he most loves. She couldn't know she'd be entangled in a web of desire, drawn to the velvet caress of Rasch's voice and the ecstatic fulfillment in his arms. You'll be thoroughly enchanted with this story of forbidden love.

The combination of love and laughter makes **MIDNIGHT KISS** by Marcia Evanick, LOVESWEPT #513, completely irresistible. To Autumn O'Neil, Thane Clayborne is a sexy stick-in-the-mud, and she delights in making him lose control. True, running a little wild is not Thane's style, but Autumn's seductive beauty tempts him to let go. Still, she's afraid that the man who bravely sacrificed a dream for another's happiness could never care for a woman who ran scared when it counted most. Another winner from Marcia Evanick!

With his tight jeans, biker boots, and heartbreak-blue eyes, Michael Hayward is a **TEMPTATION FROM THE PAST,** LOVESWEPT #514, by Cindy Gerard. January Stewart has never seen a sexier man, but she knows he's more trouble that she can handle. Intrigued by the dedicated lawyer, Michael wants to thaw January's cool demeanor and light her fire. Is he the one who would break down her defenses and cast away her secret pain? Your heart will be stirred by this touching story.

A fitting final course is **JUST DESSERTS** by Theresa Gladden, LOVESWEPT #515. Caitlin MacKenzie has had it with being teased by her new housemate, Drew Daniels, and she retaliates with a cream pie in his face! Pleased that serious Caitie has a sense of humor to match her lovely self, Drew begins an ardent pursuit. She would fit so perfectly in the future he's mapped out, but Catie has dreams of her own, dreams that could cost her what she has grown to treasure. A sweet and sexy romance—what more could anybody want?

FANFARE presents four truly spectacular books this month! Don't miss bestselling Amanda Quick's **RENDEZVOUS.** From London's most exclusive club to an imposing country manor, comes this provocative tale about a free-thinking beauty, a reckless charmer, and a love that defied all logic. **MIRACLE,** by beloved LOVESWEPT author Deborah Smith, is the unforgettable contemporary romance of passion and the collision of worlds, where a man and a woman who couldn't have been more different learn that love may be improbable, but never impossible.

Immensely talented Rosalind Laker delivers the exquisite historical **CIRCLE OF PEARLS.** In England during the days of plague and fire, Julia Pallister's greatest test comes from an unexpected quarter—the man she calls enemy, a man who will stop at nothing to win her heart. And in **FOREVER**, by critically acclaimed Theresa Weir, we witness the true power of love. Sammy Thoreau had been pronounced a lost cause, but from the moment Dr. Rachel Collins lays eyes on him, she knows she would do anything to help the bad-boy journalist learn to live again.

Happy reading!

With every good wish for a holiday filled with the best things in life,

Nita Taublib

Nita Taublib
Associate Publisher/LOVESWEPT
Publishing Associate/FANFARE

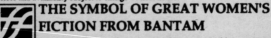

"Funny and heartrending . . . wonderful characters . . . I
laughed out loud and couldn't stop reading. A splendid
romance!" -- *Susan Elizabeth Phillips, <u>New York Times</u>*
bestselling author of FANCY PANTS and HOT SHOT

Miracle

by

Deborah Smith

An unforgettable story of love and the collision of two worlds. From a shanty in the
Georgia hills to a television studio in L.A.,
from the heat and dust of Africa to glittering
Paris nights -- with warm, humorous, passionate characters, MIRACLE weaves a spell
in which love may be improbable but never
impossible.